LEVELS
OF
CONSCIOUSNESS

LEVELS OF CONSCIOUSNESS

Short Stories

MARK SICHERMAN

iUniverse, Inc.
New York Lincoln Shanghai

LEVELS OF CONSCIOUSNESS
Short Stories

iUniverse books may be ordered through booksellers or by contacting:

iUniverse
2021 Pine Lake Road, Suite 100
Lincoln, NE 68512
www.iuniverse.com
1-800-Authors (1-800-288-4677)

Because of the dynamic nature of the Internet, any Web addresses
or links contained in this book may have changed
since publication and may no longer be valid.

This is a work of fiction. All of the characters, names, incidents, organizations,
and dialogue in this novel are either the products of the author's imagination
or are used fictitiously.

ISBN: 978-0-595-45719-9 (pbk)
ISBN: 978-0-595-70187-2 (cloth)
ISBN: 978-0-595-90020-6 (ebk)

Printed in the United States of America

To my patients, who taught me to speak their language.

Contents

Introduction

Madness or Medicine. That was the title of a workshop I attended many years ago on the island of Martha's Vineyard. I have always used any excuse to let the Vineyard work its magic on me, especially in those days when I was attempting to juggle child rearing, farm management, and a full-time medical practice.

The "madman" was Dr. Shyam S. Singha, a London-based physician, acupuncturist, classical homeopath, and naturopath. Shyam was a handsome, powerful man in his early seventies. When he looked at you, you felt understood and cared for, even as he was shattering your illusions about what it means to be a healer. He would quote chapter and verse from textbooks of medicine and psychiatry, dismiss them with an impatient wave of the hand, and then show us new ways to think about the patient's problem. In the first hour, I was hooked. My practice would never be the same.

Shyam was not my only mentor. Had I not had several prior and unconventional influences on the course of my career and personal life, I would not have been ready for Dr. Singha's unique brand of irreverent nurturing.

Dr. Alexander Lowen, the charismatic founder of the Institute for Bioenergetic Analyis and his disciples at the New York Society for Bioenergetic Analysis took me apart and put me back together again over the course of five years. Finally, at the age of fifty, I became a man, and—not incidentally—a certified bioenergetic therapist.

Dr. Herbert Benson, the true and largely unsung hero of mind-body medicine, showed me how it was possible to keep one foot firmly planted in the science of medicine while taking a bold step into ancient healing modalities (notably meditation), and apply these techniques in patient care.

Spiritual aspects of healing have become important to me in recent years. Meditation, the writings of spiritual masters, and my *sanga* have all facilitated whatever spiritual growth I have been able to attain. However, the most profound influence on that aspect of my personal and professional life came from a man who never used the word "spiritual," at least in my presence—Marvin Skorman, the therapist's psychotherapist. Awareness and acceptance of one's own true nature is, in my opinion, a prerequisite for helping others to find their path. It may even be what compassion, that much used and abused word, is all about. If I have succeeded in finding a measure of compassion for my real-life patients and for the more-real-than-life characters in these stories, I owe much of that success to Marvin.

I know all the folks in these tales, know them well. I know those doctors, the good ones and the bad ones. Or should I say the ones who are helpful and those who are not. Some of them are me. I know those patients. Some of them are me. Might I run into one of them on the street? No, because they don't exist in real life, not even the ones that *are* me. Truth, it has been said too often, is stranger than fiction. I agree. But fiction contains more truth than real life. I believe you'll see what I mean when you read these stories.

The events in the title story, *Levels of Consciousness (1959)*, really did happen in our family when I was a young intern. You might imagine that those occurrences had a profound impact on me at the time. However, you'd be wrong. I would not understand, on any level, the significance of those events until decades later. I had, back then, despite my considerable competence, no compassion for myself, my family, or my patients. Beware of young doctors.

Why did I write these stories?

When I was young, I loved to write rhyming poems and florid love letters to my girlfriends. In medical school we learned to elicit a complete history from the patient and to record it in detail in the chart. For no good reason other than pleasure, I strove for perfection in my clinical notes. My writing languished in my middle years, but in my late fifties I attended a creative writing workshop (on Martha's Vineyard!) given by Nancy Slonim Aronie. I was hooked again. A few years later, I semiretired so that I could devote some serious time to writing.

But why *these* stories?

I believe in the power of our thoughts and our emotions to make us sick. I also believe in the *healing* power of our thoughts and emotions. A considerable body of research supports both of these statements. If I were more of a scientist, I would be drawn to writing nonfiction works about these matters. But I have been a clinician for forty years and continue to be enthralled by the stories my patients tell me. I want to share those stories with others (with you, dear readers) in a way that protects the confidentiality of my patients, yet reveals the secrets behind their falling ill, or getting well, or, sometimes, dying.

I believe there are important truths in these fictions and lessons to be learned. Hopefully, they will also entertain you.

Coronary Care

The nursing staff was gathered behind the large desk, in the process of changing shifts, leaving the anesthetized body of Frank Dulcegelati in the care of the life-monitoring and life-sustaining machines of the cardiac intensive care unit. Rachael was there also, holding on to her husband's big right hand, the only appendage available to her. She smiled down at him, her compassion for his helpless state smoothing away the lines of bitterness around her mouth. Life with Frankie had not been easy for her, at least for the past twenty years, maybe never. She wondered if this near-death experience would change him; she had read about such things in women's magazines.

A young man in green surgical scrubs approached the bed.

"Mrs. Dulcegelati?" he asked. "I'm Dr. Hsima, Dr. Pendarek's resident. Everything went fine during the procedure. We wound up doing a quintuple bypass. There was more blockage than we had anticipated. Dr. Pendarek will call you himself tonight, but, between you and me," Hsima leaned closer to Rachael and whispered, "we've never seen a heart so blocked up."

Hsima turned his attention to the machines. Apparently satisfied, he asked Rachael to step behind the curtain while he removed the endotracheal tube.

"He's able to breathe on his own now," he said.

Rachael thanked the surgery resident and resumed her vigil.

"Did you hear what he said, Frankie? I guess we're lucky you're alive. Listen, I'm going to go and call Frannie to tell her you're okay. I'll be back soon. Maybe you'll be awake by then."

With this, Frank Dulcegelati opened his eyes and looked around the room. Then he looked at his wife, then at her watch. He spoke. "Rae, you feed Princess before you left the house?"

"Frankie, you kill me. You just got through a quintuple bypass, and you ask me if I fed the dog! Hey, would I forget? I know what makes you happy."

Rachael saw that are-you-*sure*-you-fed-her look on his face, the look that she usually returned with spiteful eyes and a resigned sigh. But seeing him helpless this way moved her and secretly pleased her, so she reassured him with a sweet and gentle nod of her head and a slight squeeze of his hand. She watched as the furrow between his eyebrows smoothed. His eyes closed and he began to snore softly.

✳   ✳   ✳   ✳

Knowing the dog was fed was not the only thing that made Frank Dulcegelati happy. In fact, happy was not even the right word. Relieved—the relief that comes from knowing that another of life's responsibilities had been discharged, as if someday, when all of them had been seen to, happiness might be possible. There were moments of happiness with the dog, but no one besides Frank, and possibly Princess, knew about them. Sometimes, alone with her, he would hug the dog and tell her how much he loved her. Tears of happiness would come to his eyes, tears that he would wipe away on his sleeve, glancing around to be sure no one had seen.

What else?

Opera, especially coloratura arias by Puccini and Verdi. Saturday afternoons, if no one else was at home, he would tune to *Live from the Met*, and he would sing along, until his voice grew husky with emotion and broke into a sob.

Eating at Giovanni's, with the guys from work. A glass of wine, but especially the *pasta alla Caroma*, would loosen his tongue. His eyes shone. He told jokes from eighth grade, slipping into an exaggerated Sicilian dialect and waving his arms like a conductor, until he had eaten too much (from the sheer pleasure of it, not from greed), and he grew sleepy.

And the ocean. Once a year, on vacation for a week at his brother-in-law's cottage on the North Shore, away from work and from the burdens of maintaining a home and family, he grew lighter. He swam and walked the beach and made sculptures of smooth stones in the sand.

Pendarek called Rachael at home that evening to tell her how successful the surgery had been, that Frank was doing well and would be discharged in a few days. He expected that Frank would be back to his old self, as good as new, he said, within four to six weeks, certainly by the New Year. Rachael thanked the doctor in the brightest voice she could manage, then hung up the phone and stared blankly at the darkened TV screen. Princess came over and nuzzled Rachael's left hand, looking up at her expectantly. Rachael snatched her hand away as if she had been bitten, and turned sideways on the sofa.

"Please, please, just leave me be—just for a little while," she said quietly.

*   *   *   *

Just as the doctor had predicted, by the New Year Frank was able to return to work. Everyone agreed that he seemed like his old self. But in late March, Frank's crew was repairing a downed power line on the west side of town, near the reservoir. As Dutch VanderBogen, the lineman, told it later to the charge nurse in the ER, and still later to Rachael, Dutch was up in the cherry picker with Al, Gonzoles was in the truck on the radio, and Frankie was standing next to the vehicle, making notes in the logbook. They still had three more outages to repair before they could break for lunch. Dutch said he looked down just in time to see Frankie stumble forward, then backward, falling to the pavement. The logbook slid underneath the truck.

"I thought he slipped on the ice," Dutch said.

"A massive coronary," Pendarek told Rachael. "It's hard to believe, only four months after the bypass, but his arteries are 90 percent occluded again. The worst is, I can't risk another bypass; his heart just won't stand it. We'll have to manage him with medications and hope that he recovers sufficiently to qualify for a transplant, though frankly, at his age …"

Frank's recuperation at home was slow. Progress on a daily basis was minimal, barely noticeable. Frank was too weak to care about whether the dog was fed, or the heat turned down, or the hedges trimmed.

Rachael's life was a lot easier than it had been in years. She was not happy, at least as far as anyone knew, but it was said she looked better than she had for a long time, eating well and putting on a little weight. She was a devoted nursemaid to Frank, and, like some women in that role, she was in charge, giving orders, telling him what he could or could not do, all in the interest of getting him better. She fed and petted Princess without resentment or bitterness.

From time to time, Rachael would pause in her routine, carry a chair over next to Frankie's recliner and make small talk for a while, usually about the children or gossip she'd heard at the market. She wanted to say more but was not experienced at such things. One day in late April, she asked him a question.

"So, Frankie, all this …" she waved her hand around at the walker, the commode, his half-eaten lunch on the nightstand next to an array of pharmaceuticals. "What do you think?"

Frank looked at her with the sad eyes of a man who knows he is dying. "Pain in the ass," he said. "Hey, Rae, bring me the phone, will ya, I want to call Dutch in the truck. They're over by the new mall, and I forgot to remind him about the buried cable under North Seventh."

When his wife left the room, Frank finished his secret, silent prayer to St. Lucy, his mother's favorite saint. "Just help me with a second chance, and I promise to get it right."

By June, Frank had regained enough strength to be able to bathe himself, and he usually got dressed for the day. Dr. Pendarek, after reviewing the latest cardiac function tests, was guarded in his prognosis. "A year at least," he told Rachael, "before we can even think about a transplant."

He encouraged short walks and a change of scenery. When Rachael suggested to Frank that they plan an overnight visit to his sister's home, Frank wondered if that meant she thought he would die soon.

But June had always been Frank's favorite month. He had an image of driving through the dappled green of the Berkshires in the late spring sunshine and of the wide Cotter's Mill stream rushing through the woods behind Nina's house. He agreed to go.

Rachael drove the Econoline van, which Frank had personally customized a few years back, before all the kids were grown and gone. Now he lay back in the reclining passenger seat, his feet propped on the dash. He noticed the accumulation of dust on the vent cowls and the grit in the wells of the cup holders. He wished Frank Junior was still at home to clean the van properly; Rachael could never get it right. She noticed him noticing and commented on the passing foliage, asking Frank when he thought the sugar maples would be fully leafed out.

"Another week or two," said Frank, "at least at this elevation. In Cotter's Mills they'll be full out right now."

Frank had insisted they take Route 20 through the Lebanon Valley and the Berkshires, avoiding the Mass Pike. In his younger days he had been foreman of a line crew out of Pittsfield and had upgraded the service along thirty-five miles or so of the Boston Post Road, as they called it back then. He would have liked to have stopped and inspected some of the linkages close-up, but he knew if he stood up he'd have to pee, thanks to the diuretic, and he didn't feel up to hiking off into the woods.

They detoured off Route 20 to have lunch at a diner in Lee that Frank remembered as having the best grilled cheese and bacon. The stainless exterior was unchanged, as were the marble counter and vinyl booths that Frank passed on his way to the bathrooms. The men's room was now unisex, with no urinal, and it was spotless, smelling of fake forest. He exited the bathroom thinking about the grilled cheese and feeling hungry for the first time in weeks. He found Rae in a booth near a window and sat down heavily across from her. The menu in front of him read, "Whole Earth Foods." Rachael saw his face darken.

"Hey, Frankie, it was your choice. Look, it says here, 'heart healthy.' Just pretend you're with Frannie—wouldn't *she* be in seventh heaven." Frank was soothed simply by the mention of his youngest daughter. He ordered a grilled tofu with sprouts on pita, perhaps in her honor.

An hour and a half later, they took a left off the state road and headed down County Route 202 toward North Winster. Rachael found a field of wildflowers in full bloom, stopped, and left Frank to doze in the van while she gathered armfuls for her sister-in-law. From North Winster they took a nameless shortcut and in five minutes were on Upper Main Street in Cotter's Mills.

"Do you want to stop to see Pop now, or wait until after we get settled at Nina's?" Rachael looked over at Frank who was gripping the dash with both hands hard enough that his knuckles showed white and hard beneath his skin.

"Later, later. Don't even go by the store. Take Fairview over to Nina's. Next right."

Nina, Anthony, and their youngest, Joey, still in high school, ran out to the van to greet them. Nina, crying and laughing, hugged her big brother then stepped back and looked at him with some amazement, saying, "You're here. You're really here."

Since it was an easy half-day's drive between their two houses, and since his sister had not bothered to visit him during his endless illness, Frank knew she was commenting on the fact that he was still above ground. He patted her shoulder and shook hands with his brother-in-law, who was wearing a look of fearful concern. Anthony stepped gingerly around Frank and ordered Joey to carry everything into the house. "Don't let Uncle Frankie carry anything. You understand?"

In the house, Nina apologized for not having the guest room ready, explaining that she wasn't sure if her brother was allowed to climb stairs and perhaps should sleep on the pullout in the living room. Anthony nodded vigorously and looked to Rachael for an answer.

Frank whistled loudly through his teeth like he used to when they were kids. "The guest room," he said, pointing to the stairs. "Joey will carry me up. Right, kid?"

He grinned at his nephew and started up the stairs, taking his duffel with him. Frank actually felt a lot better than he thought he would. He couldn't wait to open the guest room window wide and listen to the Cotter's Mills stream hurrying by on its way to the Housatonic. He washed up and went back downstairs. The others had decided that there was plenty of time left before dinner for Joey to drive Frank over to see Pop, and Frank had to agree that he might as well get it over with. He also figured they needed time to talk behind his back about "how long" and "what if," and other things they could never say with him there.

Anthony walked his brother-in-law out to the car. "Listen, Frankie," he said, "if you can get Pop's attention, see if you can talk him into giving up the store. He won't listen to nobody else." He patted Frank on the shoulder. "In any case, you'll want to get outa there before five, 'cause that's when the aide comes to take him back to the apartment, and she'll talk your ear off."

*   *   *   *

Frank told Joey to park the car half a block up from the store and gave him five dollars to spend at McAllister's.

"The ice cream parlor closed when I was still in grade school, Uncle Frank. I think I better just stay in the car." Joey slouched down in the seat and pulled his cap low.

Frank got out of the car and looked around. In addition to McAllister's, several other stores had been boarded up: Nigel's Hardware, Zenith Books, The Fiddle Shop. Others had been taken over by businesses he did not recognize. There was a check cashing storefront where the cigar store once stood, a Daisy Donuts where The Tackle Shop (or maybe it was DeVaul's Menswear) used to be. Both banks, the massive Mill City Savings and the Cotter's Mills branch of Worcester Trust, across from each other on the corner of South Main and Fifth Street, now stood in an eerie, stony silence, and despite the sun reflecting off their gilded roofs, looked cold.

He walked farther down the block, past a takeout taco joint— open but empty at this time of day—and past a few more boarded up stores until he stood in front of what used to be Gertie's Lunch. He tried to peek through a crack between the boards covering the front door to see if the lunch counter was still intact. Gertie had made the world's best meat loaf, which he had eaten every Saturday during the twenty minutes Pop gave him for his lunch break. He tried to remember what she served with it. Mashed potatoes? Or was it potato salad? He tried harder to find a crack in the plywood, as if seeing into the tiny eatery would help him remember. He realized he was avoiding turning around and looking across the street. He sighed and turned.

The late afternoon sunlight, funneled through a narrow vacant lot between Gertie's and the next building, illuminated the front of his father's store. The entire width of the two-story brick building was divided horizontally by the red, white, and green tiles that spelled out Salvatore Dulcegelati and Sons. Above the sign, the apartment that was rented out, usually to a family newly arrived from the old country. Below the sign, the entrance to the store, flanked on each side by the plate glass storefront windows. The left one read, Grocery, and the right, Imports, both signs hand lettered in a gold leaf arc.

The front door was open. The old man sat in the doorway on a straight-backed wooden chair. He was wearing a white shirt buttoned at the neck and a black suit, white socks, and house slippers. One hand rested on the curved handle of a cane, the other palm up in his lap. His closed eyes took in the warm sun and occasionally blinked. There was no other movement. A yellow cat lay sleeping in the window that said Imports. In the other window was a pyramid constructed of a dozen or more twenty-four-ounce cans of DeCeccho whole plum tomatoes so thick with dust that the labels could no longer be read. Frank had placed them there himself on a Saturday morning in August 1963. There was nothing else in either window and nothing on any of the hardwood shelves that lined the walls of the store and nothing in the rows of metal bins that ran down the center aisle. On the high counter near the door, the ornate brass cash register sat with its drawer open, the white figures, $0.79, showing the last purchase.

Frank squeezed past the old man and stood in the cool interior. His father seemed unaware that anyone had entered.

"Pop, it's me, Frankie," Frank said, standing behind the chair and inclining his body slightly toward the old man's head and speaking sotto voce. He knew that he would not be heard even if he was yelling directly into his father's ear, but he always tried this approach first. Rattling the chair, shaking the old man's shoulder, touching his face—these were the ways the others got Pop's attention, but it always caused Frank a sad discomfort to see the startled look on his face and to hear the gasped words in Italian. Frank tried his next move: he stomped around heavily in the vicinity of the chair, and when he heard the guttural sounds *"che? cosi e?"* he slipped around to the front of the chair and squatted down so his face would be in front of the old man's. The one good eye was open and was, perhaps, looking in his direction.

"Frankie, Frankie," his father said, his hand making an attempt to reach his son's face, but falling back uselessly into his lap.

"Yeah, I'm here, Pop. It's okay."

The old man shut his eye and sighed. He became still again, quiet in the warm sun, attending to his reveries. Frank left the store and walked back to the car, remembering other times. He saw himself in his bedroom at the old house, felt in his belly the dread he had experienced at the sound of his father's approaching footsteps. He would shrivel in anticipation of another task to be assigned, another criticism of his behavior or his appearance or his work. The old man had condemned laughter as frivolous. He had allowed no time for love. Frank remembered his mother's eyes trying to soften for her son the hard edge of his father's presence.

"How's he doing today, Uncle Frank?" asked Joey on the drive back to the house.

"Good, good, kid. He'll probably live forever." *Only the good die young*, he thought.

Dinner was uncomfortable. Talk about illness was carefully avoided. Frank asked about the other siblings, but Nina and Anthony knew even less than he did. Perhaps this one still lives in Miami, or maybe that one has a new wife. Any closeness that might have existed among the kids had evaporated when their mother died. And they did not talk about life before her death. During dessert, Joey said that he wished he had known his grandmother.

"What was she like, Uncle Frankie? You must've known her best, being the oldest boy and all. Ma says you were Grandma's favorite."

Frank responded with a fit of coughing and became quite red faced. The others bustled with concern, but Frank waved them off, pushed away the ricotta pie and excused himself from the table. From the front room he could hear Rachael.

"Joey, your uncle never talks about his mom. He says he doesn't remember, but between you and me ..." Rachael's voice dropped too low for Frank to hear the rest.

After breakfast the next morning, Frank offered to drive Joey to school while the sisters-in-law did the dishes. Joey, remembering his father's admonition not to cause Frankie any *agita,* told his uncle that he didn't mind the mile walk, especially on such a nice day, but Frank insisted. On the way, Frank asked Joey if he knew whether the old high school was still used for something. Joey explained that it had been converted to an old peoples' home, complete with wheelchair ramps and a garden where the basketball court used to be. Frank shook his head.

Frank dropped Joey at the side entrance to the "new high school" and headed back downtown to check out his old alma mater. The day was warming up fast, and as he pulled into the parking lot of Old School Manor, several of the residents were already sunning themselves on benches in the garden. He walked over and sat on a bench facing two older ladies, well dressed and chatty, who squinted into the sun to get a better look at him, asking him if he was a new resident.

"Well, no," Frank said, a bit too emphatically. "I used to go to high school here."

"We did too, dear, didn't we, Alma," said the less wrinkled one. "I was class of '43 and Alma here was '41. What about you?"

"Ahh ...'52, 1952," said Frank, quickly calculating the difference in ages between himself and the old ladies, which, seen from this perspective, was distressingly small. Then, remembering his heart condition, he thought, *I should be so lucky.* Old School Manor did not seem such a bad place.

"Have you been over to the old elementary school, Mr....?"

"Frank, just call me Frank." He did not want to have to explain about Pop and the store.

"Well, Frank, you should go. Right, Alma?"

"It's quite a sight," said the older old woman.

Frank thanked them and left. Before getting back in the van, he walked around to the side of the building to see if it still said Boys over the entrance. It did. He assumed it also still said Girls on the other side but didn't feel up to the walk.

Frankie recalled that the old elementary school was in that part of town known as the East End. It was just a few blocks from the house where he was born and where the family had lived until Frankie was in the fourth grade. But right now he couldn't think how to drive there. There had never been any reason to go back to the East End. Nina had recently referred to its current inhabitants as coming from places in the world she had never even heard of.

Frankie drove the van back to Main Street and headed east. He considered stopping at the new Mobil Mini-Mart and asking directions, but to where? "Excuse me, can you tell me how to get to the old elementary school?" No, he'd find it on his own. When he got to the corner of Seventh and Main, he looked north, and it seemed familiar. He turned left and drove slowly up Seventh. He found the old school on the corner of Union Street, across from the old orphanage, now a deserted branch library.

It was indeed a sight. Little more than the front and the south side of the building still stood, its windows boarded up, lifeless, bearing ancient grafitti. One said, "Stop the War." A construction fence was around the open sides, to keep the kids out, he supposed, but would have been but a minor deterrent to any determined teen. Through the fence, Frank could see the broken urinals in the basement. He was pretty sure they didn't make urinals that small anymore.

Frank remembered walking to school hand in hand with Lucca, his oldest sister who died of heart failure within a year after Mom's death. Lucca would shoo him inside the door of Miss Garroway's kindergarten class, first making sure his hair was combed and that he had his milk money in his pants pocket. Even before they left the house, Lucca would give him the once-over, seeing to it that his shirt was tucked in and his brown and whites securely tied.

"Jeet, Frankie? You know Mom will kill you if she finds out if you din't have breakfast."

Frank had an image of the two of them, Lucca and himself, standing just inside the back door of the old house, the kitchen door that led to the back porch. They could hear Mom upstairs, singing to the twins while she bathed and changed them and yelling to little Carm to bring her a diaper pin or the cornstarch. Frank tried to recall the front of the house, but images of more recent homes kept intruding. He felt a tightening in his belly, just below his rib cage, and wondered if he had eaten too many of Nina's pancakes.

Suddenly it became very important to Frankie to find the old house. He couldn't have said why, but there was an urgency about it that one could not question. He started to walk in the direction of the house but then realized he didn't know where it was anymore. His belly felt worse, and he thought maybe he should get back in the van. But he needed to see that house. He walked north to the next corner where the candy store used to stand. He remembered that on the way to school they had approached the candy store from the side, so he turned the corner and headed east, past rundown houses that looked vaguely familiar. At the next corner, the street sign said East Division, and the number eighty-two popped into his head. Eighty-two East Division. Breathless, half running now in what he knew was the right direction, he saw the front of the house in his mind's eye before he reached it.

Now he saw and remembered the big wraparound front porch, its former skewed wooden stairs replaced by an ugly but more serviceable set of precast concrete, complete with wrought iron railings on both sides. He stood on the sidewalk, keeping a respectful distance, and tried to look up at the first and second story windows, squinting his eyes against the morning sun. He thought his room, his and Angelo's, might have been the one on the right, above the porch roof. Did he and Angelo, five and seven, actually climb out on that roof and slide down the porch support column on a day much like today? Now it seemed very important to try to reach Angelo (New York? Brooklyn?)

to check out the facts. He saw the two of them. They were running cross-lots to Anthony Mazzulo's to play mumblety-peg in his back yard because no adults were there to yell at them about the knives.

But the inside. Frank couldn't "see" inside the house no matter how hard he willed his brain to remember. His belly tightened more. His chest ached. He thought he should walk away, let it go. It felt dangerous. Yet it had been a very long time since he'd wanted anything as badly as he now wanted to see the inside of the house. *Walk up the steps and ring the goddam bell,* he thought. He had an image of an unshaven man in an undershirt opening the door and yelling "Whaddya want, kid? Get outa here!"

A young woman in a smock and a babushka came around the side of the house, carrying a yellow plastic trashcan with a cracked lid. She set the can on the curb and looked down the street at the neighbor's garbage and then looked at Frank.

"Sir, maybe perhaps is something I can help with you?"

Why is she calling me sir? Frank thought. He said in a small voice, "I think this is my house."

"Used to be living here? That's nice. Come, come inside. See for yourself. I am Irina. Is only me and my Uncle Dimitri living here. Is okay with him too."

Frank let himself be led up the front steps and into the dark foyer. The house smelled of cooking. Not Mama's sauce, but pleasant just the same. His belly relaxed a little. He felt a bit dizzy. He thought he heard a small boy's voice—"Ma, I'm home."

There was a curved staircase with a polished mahogany banister off to the left. Uninvited, he began climbing the steps, slowly at first, then faster, almost running, effortlessly, knowing she'd be there. At the top, he turned left and walked directly through the open door of a room at the end of the short hallway.

Sunlight streamed through the east-facing window, creating an aura around the silhouetted form of a woman and the baby she held in her arms.

"Carissimo. My baby Frankie. I love you so much."

Frankie stood transfixed, his arms reaching toward the open window, his shoulders heaving. A small boy's voice said, "Mama, Mama." He felt the touch of a hand on his back, soft and warm. He turned and sank to his knees, wrapping his arms around Irina's waist, clinging, his head pressed to her bosom.

Frank, his man's voice now broken by sobs, repeating, "Mama ... I love you ... I love you ..."

Slowly, when he was ready, Irina helped him to his feet. Frank was laughing now, occasionally crying, struggling to explain and apologize. She soothed him, patted his hand. Together they descended the curved staircase and passed through a narrow hall into the kitchen. She made him a cup of tea, and they drank together, talking about the weather. After a while Frank began smiling broadly and shifted restlessly in his chair, like a teenager with someplace to go.

Irina led him out the front door and wished him well, telling him to return anytime. She watched as Frank bounded down the steps and ran to the corner, turning right, retracing his steps.

Frank was in a hurry. He couldn't wait to see Rachael, to take her in his arms, to tell her how much he loved her, to tell her he was sorry and that everything was going to be all right.

✳   ✳   ✳   ✳

A week later, he was back in Pendarek's office. Rachael had insisted on it. She worried he was doing too much. Running up and down stairs, cleaning out old stuff from the attic, stuff that he had insisted on saving and now was hauling to the dump without even looking through it. He'd been making a lot of phone calls to the kids, to old buddies, joking and laughing with them, making plans to get together. He never asked her if the dog had been fed. Rachael wondered if he might have suffered brain damage. She went with him to the appointment and tried to explain these things to Pendarek while he was examining Frank and running tests and making notes in a manila folder. Finally he sat the two of them down in his consultation room.

Pendarek spoke carefully at first. "Frank, have you been getting some kind of treatment that you haven't told me about? Another doctor, or herbal remedies, or something?"

Rachael looked suspiciously at Frankie who laughed and threw up his hands.

"C'mon. You know me, Doc," he said.

"Well," said Pendarek, appearing excited, almost giddy, talking faster. "I've never seen anything like this. To be honest, I never expected your heart to recover, Frank. And now, I can't find a thing wrong with you. You have a heart like a teenager!"

"I'm just a teenager in love." Frankie sang the words. Everyone laughed.

The House
of Castleman

Helen is off to Boston again for a couple of days. I'm certain she sensed my disapproval, but at least I kept quiet about it. She tells me that I grow "even colder" as the time for her to leave approaches. I replied, with an unintended hint of sarcasm, that I would "reflect" on this while she was away.

Sadly, I must admit that after seventy-two years of existence, after raising two families, and, incredibly, after forty years as a physician, I have never really touched another human heart. Human, I say, because the feeling I have for my dogs, for each one of that series of large mixed-breed shepherds—Osler, Waldo, Woody, and now Ben—has come, keen as the blade of a scalpel, from a magical fissure in the sternum, that breastplate which, in the presence of Homo sapiens, seems cast in cold steel.

Note, please, and note it well, that it is the sternum, not the cor *itself, which is made of such hard stuff. I do not wish to be misunderstood. I am not hard-hearted. In fact, I'm an old softie. My heart beats warm in its cage. I can feel it. Sometimes, and even then it is only momentary, the heat of it seeks to melt the steel, intent on merging with the warmth of another heart, and, finding no escape, turns back on itself and roils around awhile. I watch with clinical detachment, wondering if I will have a heart attack, until it cools down and I feel normal again. Normal for me. Safe. I like to think that if I had a choice, if I had control of it, if I had a remote in my pocket with a button that says Open, I would risk being unsafe.*

Of course it all goes back to Mother. She was ...

The doctor is interrupted in his writing by a knock on the side entry door, the door that used to lead directly into the kitchen pantry until Helen, the doctor's wife, had the kitchen remodeled, eliminating the old pantry with the copper sink and marble drainboard, and had installed in its place a mudroom. They had argued about this, Helen adamant that she needed the room to keep the children from tracking mud into the kitchen on their sodden sneakers, the doctor reluctant to part with the essential elements of his childhood.

He closes the journal and slips it back into its place behind the ledgers in the file drawer of the oak rolltop. He goes to the window, sees no car in the driveway, and surmises the interrupter is a neighbor, a child, or a woman, because Ben did not bark. He goes down the narrow back stairs, the servants' stairs as his grandmother used to call them, through the kitchen and into the "mudroom." There has been no mud in this room, he thinks, for nearly fifteen years. He recognizes the girl through the small round window in the entry door, the bobbing pigtailed head and dark eyes coming into the frame and then disappearing.

"I'm coming," he shouts, and fumbles with the deadbolt. "Trina. Come in, child, come in."

The girl hesitates in the doorway, looks down at her shoes, and starts to kneel.

"No, no, don't worry about the sneakers, they're not muddy. Besides," he lowers his voice, "Mrs. Castleman's not home." He steps aside, motioning her in, closes the door, and sits heavily on the pine bench, searching Trina's face.

"Mama says she don't want to be a bother, but she's worried about TJ. She says to tell you he's shaking all over and got a high fever. Like to have a fit maybe."

The doctor smiles, puts his hand on the girl's thin shoulder. "Run home and tell your mama I'll be right there. I have to put on some shoes and get my bag." He rises from the chair and ascends the stairs with a lightness that Helen, had she been there, would have noticed with surprise.

When he returns to the house an hour later, he is humming a tune. "Ta-ta tee-ta, ta-ta tee-tata, sweet Georgia Brown." He sets the plate of molasses cookies, the only compensation he had been willing to accept for the house call, on the kitchen table and boils water for his midmorning tea. He carries the tea and cookies up to his study and resumes his writing.

She was … the doctor sits for a long time looking at those two words. The pen wavers in his bony hand, wagging back and forth like a finger in the face of a naughty child. His face sags, expressionless. His body seems to fold in upon itself, and he suddenly feels very sleepy. His eyes close, and perhaps he dozes for a few seconds. When he opens his eyes again, the words are still there.

She was … His jaw clenches. Suddenly he inhales deeply, rapidly, inflating his body to an erect posture in the desk chair … *an intrusive, overbearing monster. She couldn't keep her hands and her mouth off me. She wanted to consume me with her love. "I'm going to eat you up," she would say.*

I felt the truth of that statement and, fearful for my very existence, did what I could to protect my anatomy. But I was a good child, and sensitive. I knew that I also had to protect her from becoming aware of my rage, my revulsion and disgust. So I contrived acceptable methodologies to slip from her grasp. I laughed mirthlessly, pretending that I was ticklish to her touch, and wriggled myself free.

I feigned sleep, stomach aches, and sore throats. I had to tinkle or have a BM. Or I whined that I was hungry, a most effective stratagem, sending her to the kitchen to prepare a feast for her little king.

If you doubt that a small child is capable of such clever intrigue, let me reassure you that it is not only possible, but common. I have seen it time and again in my practice. The mother who complains that little Freddy won't let her kiss him. Freddy and I look at each other and we both know that the other knows. "Leave him alone," I advise. "He'll come around faster that way." I lie for the sake of the child.

He will not come around. Not for her, not for any woman, not ever. Oh, he will, in time, act as if he loves Her. He will be affectionate, considerate, and eager to copulate, thrusting his sword into Her, mercilessly. But his heart, his heart … I have already told you about his heart.

The doctor lays his pen down and rereads what he has written. He grimaces from time to time and rocks gently in the swivel chair, nodding frequently. He closes the journal and returns it to its lair. He calls to Ben who has been asleep in the adjacent bedroom, and the two of them descend the front stairs as far as the upper landing, where they pause, sit down on the step together, and look down through the crystal chandelier into the large foyer and past to the rarely used double front entry doors with their Tiffany windowpanes. The doctor sighs, stroking Ben's ears.

"You get the mail, I'll see to lunch," he says to the dog. On his way down the stairs, he pauses at the lower landing and peers into the darkened living room. "Useless," he mutters to himself, and descends the rest of the staircase. He takes the single piece of mail from Ben—a gas and electric bill—and walks back to the kitchen. He prepares his usual lunch of celery sticks, Stilton cheese, rice crackers, and a pear, and carries it into the breakfast room along with a few biscuits for Ben and a cup of tea. He looks out into the garden at Helen's award winning perennials while he eats, pausing every few bites to toss a treat to the dog. "Good boy," he says, each time.

Ben jumps up suddenly and races toward the mudroom, barking happily. In a moment he returns, followed by a tall young man in a tan poplin summer suit, carrying a leather briefcase in one hand and a MacDonald's bag in the other.

"Irradiated, hormone-laced beef on a bun," he says, holding up the bag. "Moldy potatoes deep-fried in rancid, genetically engineered soybean oil. Chocolate milk shake made from BHt, antibioticised cow's milk, and plastic ice cream."

The young man places each item on the glass-topped table, then stoops to kiss the doctor on the cheek. He looks at the doctor's nearly empty plate, then at his watch.

"Am I too late?" he says.

"Keep eating that garbage, and you'll be late all right. The late Alan Castleman. How could you be late? I didn't know you were coming. Tea?"

Alan nods. "Yes, please—black, not green."

The doctor rises, goes into the kitchen.

"Mom—Helen Mom—told me you were going to be alone for a few days. Anita wants to make dinner for you tomorrow night. Okay, Dad?"

"I'll check with my social secretary," the doctor says as he returns and places a small Haviland teapot and matching cup and saucer on the table in front of his son. "Give it three minutes."

He lays a hand on Alan's shoulder and gives it a squeeze. "I'm glad you came. Truth be told, I am a bit lonely."

He returns to his seat and grins across the table. "Chronic, recurrent loneliness of the elderly. DSM 301.9. I hear Glaxo Wellcome has a new pill for that with a smiley face on it."

"Yeah, and little hands that reach out to you. Cool. By the way, Glaxo stock's doing very well. Want me to buy you some?"

"No. I don't need more things. Conversation maybe, but no one besides me seems to have time for that these days."

He makes a stop sign with his hand in Alan's direction.

"If you say one word about 'other people your age' or mention the senior center, I'll call the police. It's against the law now to verbally abuse the elderly."

"Hey, you said a long time ago that you married Helen because she was such a great conversationalist, remember? I mean, she'll be back in couple of days, Dad."

"Your stepmother has, of late, joined the Busy Bee Club." The doctor points toward the gardens. "When she's not out there, she's at yoga class. Then there are the endless board meetings, always in the evening, of course. And the daily calls to the daughters. This crisis, that crisis. Watching her makes my head swim. It's like MTV."

Alan sighs, bounces his straw up and down in the milk shake. "Have you told Helen that you feel lonely, that you wish she'd ..."

"Don't be ridiculous, Alan. It's so clear that she's doing all this to get away from me, even if she doesn't know it. Why, it all started the day I took down the shingle. Anyway, who could blame her, the way I've been since then."

"You know, you never really told me why you retired. Your health is great, you always loved the practice, the kids, the office itself." Alan gestures toward the rear of the house. "You could still reopen it."

The cell phone in the young man's pocket rings softly. He holds up one finger in the doctor's direction while he answers. "Castleman ... ah, Estella, thanks for the reminder. Please tell the one thirty that I'll be about twenty minutes late. Act apologetic. Thanks."

The doctor looks at his watch, tosses the last biscuit to Ben, then stands and picks up the tea set. "Better get going," he says to his son.

"No way. Not until you tell me why you retired." Alan folds his arms across his chest and sits back in the chair.

The doctor stops, halfway to the kitchen, his back to his son. The Haviland cup rattles in the saucer. He turns and comes back to the table and sets the china down carefully. He remains standing, grasps the top slat of the ladder-back chair, leaning into it.

"Lots of reasons. But the last straw was the goddamn managed care. Asshole MBAs and lawyers telling me how to run my practice. Jesus Christ!"

"Dad, I've heard the Health Care Delivery lecture. I remember your last speech to the county society ... they're probably still whistling and cheering … and, you said then … you said to us, 'I'll go on practicing the way I know is best until I drop, even if I don't get paid.' So. So, why?"

Dr. Castleman's hands drop to his sides. He stares down through the glass tabletop at his son's glossy wing tips, speaking softly. "I missed a diagnosis, congenital aortic stenosis, and the kid died. I knew then it was time to go out to pasture." He continues looking down, his voice husky. "Please don't share that information."

Alan blows air noisily through his teeth. "I'm sorry, Dad. I didn't know. You must have felt terrible. I won't say a word. Thanks for telling me."

The doctor straightens and picks up the tea set. "Enough said. Get back to work before your one thirty takes his money elsewhere. I'll see you tomorrow night."

On his way out the door, Alan turns and grins. "You can talk to old Kristina tomorrow. Now there's a conversationalist."

"Wise guy," says the doctor. He laughs and snorts as the door closes.

"Ben," he says, "has Kristina ever talked to you? Osler told me that she spoke to him, once. 'Move,' she said, 'so I can vacuum.' Come on, let's go around the block."

After his walk, the doctor takes a nap in the heavily shaded guest room, coming awake and alert after exactly twenty minutes, then returns to his journal writing in the study.

I hated to lie to Alan, but the explanation seemed to satisfy him. Besides, I may have missed a congenital co-arc; nearly every pediatrician does at least once in his career. What choice did I have except to lie? How could I tell him, or anyone, about the tears. The foolish breaking down into sobs in front of the mother and baby. If it had only happened once, I would have ignored it, made some excuse, gone on with my work. But it began to happen nearly every day. A young mother, gazing down at her child with this pure love, and the baby in her arms, safe, looking up at her, his face radiant, joyful. I tried to look away, to not see, as it were, but

I was drawn to the vision, part of me hoping for the chance each day. Crazy. Crazy old fool. I had to get out.

Alan is a joy to have as a son. I'll have to try talking to old Kristina tomorrow, just so I can report back to Alan. Every Wednesday for what, forty years, and never a peep from her. What stories there must be in that old head, under that babushka.

Helen will be back tomorrow, or is it Thursday? Knowing her, she probably said Wednesday or Thursday, being unable to predict how long it would take to shepherd Laura through the massive trauma of moving to a new apartment around the corner. Bah, humbug. I am an old Scrooge, but really! Anyway, I'll be glad to have her home. I wonder if she knows that.

That evening, the doctor goes to bed as usual, after the ten o'clock news. Ben is on the floor at the side of the bed, waiting for morning.

The doctor is awakened by a narrow shaft of early morning sun entering horizontally through a crack in the venetian blinds, and shining directly in his left eye. *My Lord*, he thinks, *I've slept through the night without peeing. Will wonders never cease?* Then he hears a soft, impatient tapping on the bedroom door and for a moment freezes, until he realizes that Ben has not barked.

"Come in, come in," he shouts.

The door squeaks open partway, and an old face, framed by a black kerchief, peers in at him.

"Ah, Kristina, you gave me a start. Is something the matter?" *Well, well, he thinks, she's never knocked on this door before; she's going to have to speak now. What on earth could she want?*

The old woman steps quickly into the room and closes the door firmly behind her. She walks slowly to the bedside, displacing Ben, and sits, turning her body to face the doctor. She smiles; the doctor watches, fascinated, as her wrinkles fade away, her eyes soften and shine, her mouth becomes full and moist, her teeth perfect. She raises her left hand and slips off the black babushka, shaking her head side to side, releasing a torrent of fragrant, shiny black curls. She smiles again at the doctor and places her right hand on his thigh. His body stiffens, then softens under her hand as she gently strokes his flesh through the soft summer quilt. Slowly, her hand moves higher, continues stroking. The doctor moans softly and turns his head to the side. The woman uses her left hand now to gently bring the doctor's face to meet hers. She leans closer, strokes faster and harder. She moistens her lips as if to speak, then mouths the words, "I'm going to eat you up."

The doctor sits bolt upright in bed, drenched in sweat, his mouth in a silent scream. The room is dark. He hears Ben restless on the floor, whining softly. He leans over, switches on the bed lamp, looks at his watch. Midnight. He gets out of bed, goes into the adjoining study, and records the dream in his journal.

Back in bed, he lies there for a very long time, staring at the ceiling. At three a.m., he says aloud, "This is useless," and gets out of bed, goes downstairs, and fixes himself a cup of warm milk and honey, which he carries back upstairs to the study. He sips the drink as he reads his journal, skipping over some pages, rereading others carefully. As time passes, he begins to shift in his chair, scratch his head, stomp his bare foot on the floor as if to kill an insect. He rises abruptly, snatches up the open journal, and heaves it across the room. "This is USELESS," he screams.

The doctor moves swiftly. He picks up the journal and marches with it through the upstairs hall into the front room, formerly his mother's bedroom. A brass plate on the door says Helen's Hideaway. Like the living room below it, Helen's office has a fireplace. Helen never uses it. The doctor crumples up several sheets of newspaper and starts a fire. He finds an old cardboard box, tears it to pieces, and adds this to the blaze. He tosses in the journal and, without a second glance, leaves the room, slamming the door.

"Good," he says.

He goes into the bathroom, pees, swallows two sleeping pills with a half glass of water, and walks to his bedroom. He hears Ben whine.

"You might as well go out in the yard, old fella. It's almost morning, and I want to sleep in."

He takes the dog downstairs and lets him out into the small fenced yard between the house and the office. He returns to bed and falls asleep immediately.

*   *   *   *

Some hours later, he comes half-awake in a barbiturate haze, waking and dozing, his mouth dry, his eyes burning. He thinks he hears sirens coming closer and tries to get out of bed but falls asleep again, propped against the headboard. Moments later he hears an amplified male voice calling him.

"Dr. Castleman. Dr. Castleman, can you hear me?"

He is confused, doubting the reality of the voice, thinks perhaps he is dreaming again. Then he smells the smoke. He gets out of bed, staggers toward the bedroom door, but wheels around when he hears the north window shatter. First a ladder, then a helmeted head appears through the broken glass. The fireman knocks away the shards of glass remaining in the frame, then calls to him.

"Doc, your house is on fire. Hurry. Follow me. I'll guide you down the ladder." The fireman speaks urgently but softly, as if they were planning some illegal escape.

The doctor follows, his head reeling. He wonders if he will fall from the ladder to his death, but it is only a thought. He is not afraid.

"Wait," he says. "The dog. My dog."

"He's outside, he's fine, I promise. Let's get out of here." The fireman climbs through the window and descends partway down the ladder. Then he extends his hand to the doctor and guides him onto the ladder, keeping his body pressed against the old man, his arms on either side of him.

The doctor hears a woman's voice screaming up at him from the street, hysterical. "Henry. Thank God. Henry, be careful. Oh, please God. Henry!"

He tries to shout, to reassure her, but cannot. He mutters to the fireman, "Tell my wife I'm okay. Tell her I'll be right down."

The fireman makes no response; he continues to support the doctor during their slow descent onto the grass of the small side yard.

Henry hears Helen's voice again from the street, pleading, crying. "Let me go, please. He needs me."

She tries to break free from the grasp of a young fireman. As Henry, supported by his rescuer, moves toward her, the fireman releases her, and she runs to him. They hold each other for a long time, Helen weeping into her husband's shoulder, Henry gently patting her back. After a time they step back and make their way over the maze of hoses on the ground, around to the front.

Henry sees that the entire front of the house is ablaze and that now smoke has begun to pour from the window of their bedroom. He stands and watches mutely, his hands dangling uselessly, his body swaying.

"Oh, Henry, I'm so sorry. I shouldn't have left you," his wife says softly, half-clinging to him, half-propping him up. "My God, three generations of Castlemans in that house. I'm so sorry, my love. Poor Henry."

Henry hears the words … three generations of Castlemans in that house … and he suddenly remembers the dream, the burning of the journal, the sleeping pills, letting the dog outside.

"Thank God," he says. Then, as if he is in a pulpit, "Praise be to God."

"Oh, yes, Henry. You and I are safe, and together. And Ben also," she adds, seeing the dog trotting toward them.

Henry steps away from her, his eyes bright, beaming. He begins to laugh, slowly, softly, the laugh coming from somewhere in his belly. Helen mistakes it for crying and moves to comfort him. Then the laugh erupts. Loud, uncontrolled, unmistakable, raucous, devilish laughter. He faces the house squarely, looks at the inferno. He tries to speak. "Three gen—" but breaks down again in a fit of laughing. "Three genera—"

He points an accusing finger at the blazing house. "Gone! Praise the Lord!" he shouts, and again is consumed by laughter.

Helen stands watching him, her eyes wide, her hands at her mouth. She waits and watches as the laughter slowly subsides. Finally, her husband stands tall, smiling, his eyes moist, shining. She sees him extend his arms to her, reaching, open. He falters momentarily, placing his right hand on his sternum, frowning. Then the smile returns, and he embraces his wife.

"I love you, Helen. I love you so much," he says.

Handicapped

Prentiss slips off her ivory pumps and places them, precisely parallel, next to the front door. She tiptoes into the white-carpeted living room and places the vase of freshly cut Casablanca lilies on the mantle of the gas fireplace beneath and slightly to the left of the portrait of her father, Caldwell Owens Davis III. Prentiss is tall and big boned, like her father, except for her fingers, which are delicate and tapered. She has always hated her hands. She thinks they have betrayed her.

Prentiss steps back and appraises the arrangement. She shakes her head no, fiercely. "Not perfect," she hisses to the empty room. She plucks a slightly wilted petal from one of the lilies and rotates the vase ninety degrees clockwise. Dropping the petal into the pocket of her gardening apron, she steps back again, smiling now, that big, toothy smile that everyone says lights up the whole room. She takes great pleasure in the aesthetic balance created by the peaks of her father's breast-pocket *mouchoir* and the upward-reaching petals of the flowers. She sighs, relieved, and backs slowly out of the room.

She is still smiling as she accelerates the white town car onto the eastbound lane of the freeway. She glances in the rearview mirror at little Hans, securely buckled in the rear seat. He looks almost lost in the folds of pearl gray leather, but he is there. She hopes Dr. Rasheed will do what is right for the poor boy.

She remembers that Ross had tried to buy her a Saab convertible last year, when her father was still alive. It was a pretty car, she recalls, and she was tempted. She knew, however, that it was important to Buzz Davis that his family "buy American," and Ross, thank goodness, was willing to do the right thing. She couldn't bear a tiff, especially with her father so very ill. Mr. Davis also had an opinion about what to do with little Hans, which he whispered to her when Ross and her mother were out of the room.

"Big people know what's best," she says aloud, glancing again in the mirror.

Dr. Rasheed is not very big, she thinks; he is about Ross' size. Father was six-four, she remembers. She wonders if big men really have big hearts, because that's what everyone always said about him, that he was bighearted. And of course there were his big, warm hands. When she thinks this, she avoids looking at her hands, which are thin and cold and usually under cover of gloves, white calfskin in winter, white cotton in warm weather. At night she bites her hands, all around the base of her nails, until they bleed. No one knows this except Ross.

"Do you know that rats in a trap will gnaw off their own legs to escape," he said to her one time.

She exits the freeway at the university medical complex, negotiating the ramps, twists, and turns with assurance and ease. She drives like a man, but in all else she is studiously feminine. She keeps her thick black hair swept back from her face and secured with two silver barrettes. She has good bearing, as her mother has always said, and now Prentiss says it about both of her daughters, Pamela, in her second year at Sarah Lawrence and lovely Rachael, a senior at the Carlisle Academy.

"The three of you are picture perfect," her mother always says.

Prentiss frowns, thinking of her daughters now. She has never been able to understand why they don't seem to share her adoration of her father. At Buzz's funeral, Prentiss actually thought she saw

Pamela glance at Rachael and smile as the coffin was lowered into the ground. But it couldn't have been, she thinks.

Prentiss parks the car in a handicapped space near the entrance to the Developmental Evaluation Center. She does not worry about the fine she may incur by parking there without one of those dreadful blue and white wheelchair tags hanging on her windshield. She carries the silent Hans quickly from the car to the entrance, hoping no one will notice what a clumsy pair they make, Hans' useless legs dangling down to her knees and swinging to and fro as she walks.

She is relieved when Dr. Rasheed agrees that it would indeed be best for all concerned if Hans were placed at Glenora Hughes.

"He will be among many children with similar afflictions," he says, "and besides, I am the attending neurologist there and will be checking on him weekly." He accompanies Prentiss and Hans back to the car. "Such a generous man, your father," he says, gesturing toward the Center. "All that remains is for you and your husband to come in and sign the papers. Or, in this case, it can be arranged at your home, if you prefer. Speak to Mr. Hamilton and call me."

That night, at eleven o'clock, she taps softly on the door to her husband's bedroom and enters. She is wearing the negligee that Buzz Davis had brought her from Paris nearly twenty-five years ago, just before her wedding. He had insisted she model it for him, "to make sure it fits properly and is the right color for your eyes," he said.

"Ross, darling, I need to discuss something with you," she says.

Her husband removes his glasses and closes the book he is reading. He stares at her silently for a moment, then draws his breath in sharply. "You're not exactly dressed for discourse, Tissy," he says, folding back the covers.

"Oh, silly Ross, what a one-track mind you have." Prentiss crawls under the covers, lies on her back with her hands behind her head, buried in her thick hair. She closes her eyes and smiles, waiting.

Her husband, breathing hard, whispers to her. "Tissy, just this once, please touch me, please." Gently, he tries to pull one of her hands free.

"Ross, no. My hands!" She locks her hands together, the smile gone. "Just do what we always do," she says.

When it is over, she uses the bathroom. When she returns, she sees that Ross has turned on his side, away from her, covers drawn up tightly.

"We'll talk in the morning," he says. "Please turn out the light when you go."

*   *   *   *

"What did you want to discuss, dear?" he says as she pours his coffee.

Prentiss sits across from him. She is already dressed for the Community Foundation board meeting, although it is just before eight and the meeting is not until ten. She folds her hands on the table. She is wearing short, off-white kidskin gloves, just a shade darker than her silk shantung jacket.

"Dr. Rasheed says that Hans is ready for Glenora Hughes."

"My God, Prentiss, not again. I've told you, I will not warehouse my son."

"But Rasheed is a lovely man. And he's the attending neurologist at Glenora, which everyone says is a lovely place. Ross, darling, our lives are so perfect except …"

Prentiss watches helplessly as her husband quietly gets up, places his cup and saucer in the sink, and exits through the garage door. She listens as the vintage Corvette springs to life. *But father bought you that car*, she thinks.

Prentiss sits rigidly at the kitchen table, staring at her gloved hands. "I have to make this happen," she whispers. "Please help me."

Something her friend Daphne had said recently at lunch, after the garden club meeting, tumbles into Prentiss' awareness. She smiles, thinking of the always shockingly outspoken Daphne; Daphne, who once told the mayor's wife that her tulip bed was unimaginative and "hopelessly *passé*."

At lunch that day, the girls had been bemoaning the recalcitrance of husbands, all except Daphne, that is.

"I don't have that problem," she said. "At night, I am the genie let out of the vial. I turn Bennett's bedtime fantasies into reality. And by day, I am the master, or should I say mistress, of my fate—both of our fates, actually. He becomes a pussy cat, or should I say a slave to my p—Oh, dear, a little too much wine."

"You make yourself sound like a whore," said Sarah, who was president of the garden club.

"Less boring than a hor-ticulturist, my dear," Daphne said, giggling.

The rudiments of a plan begin to take form in Prentiss' mind. It had never before occurred to her that Ross might really want something more from her sexually. She knew he revered her perfect body, and she never failed to let him have his way with her when he asked. When he panted for something different (*like last night*, she thinks), she always perceived it as the mad ranting of a man in the throes of passion. She never thought that he, a grown man, could *really* want those things from her. These were not things that he should expect from her, from his dear Tissy. *Ross is a good and kind man, like Father,* she thinks, *only not as big as Father and therefore not always knowing what is best for me. Or for poor little Hans.*

"Yes, I have to make this happen." This time she says it aloud. Prentiss resolves that if Ross wants her to touch him, she will. She is sure he will not mind if she wears her gloves. *Which ones?* she wonders. *And there was something else he asked for one time,* she knows, but she cannot quite think what that might have been. "I will do that too," she says, half-aloud, "and the next day I will ask him to take me to the carousel."

She looks at the kitchen clock and realizes she will be late for her meeting. She stands up and for a moment feels dizzy and not able to recall which meeting she will be late for. She feels like she will be late for school but knows it can't be that. Then she smiles, remembering the Foundation meeting, and goes to her car.

*   *   *   *

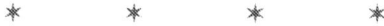

It is nearly four o'clock by the time Prentiss enters the freeway for the drive home. There was the overly long board meeting, then lunch at the Corinthian Club with Caldwell Davis' old friend Mark Van Alstyne. Mark had stroked her cheek with a lingering hand and waxed nostalgic about Buzz.

"Always kind, always gentle, and he always got what he wanted, the old fox," he laughed.

Then there was the bothersome detour to the mall to exchange Ross' new cashmere for a smaller size. *Now,* she thinks, *if I stop for groceries, I won't make it home before the special services bus.*

"The driver will simply have to wait, that's all there is to it," she says to herself.

In the business of the day, she has quite forgotten about her plan, but when she goes into Hans' room at nine o'clock to make sure he is securely in bed, she remembers. She experiences a moment of excitement—oh, the possibilities, once he is safely at Glenora Hughes—which quickly dissolves into an ill-defined vertiginous chill throughout her body.

Prentiss goes into her room and looks for her Pooh Bear pajamas. She wonders if Mommy has put them in the wash. She puts on her warm pink flannels. *He likes these too,* she thinks, *and they do make me feel a bit warmer.*

She knows she shouldn't knock on his door for another hour at least. These men work so hard. "We should do what we can to keep them happy," her mother used to say. She tries to read *Gardens Illustrated,* then gives it up for *Vogue,* but finds both of them boring. They make her sleepy. *I would get in my bed and go to sleep right now,* she thinks, *if he wasn't counting on me to come in and kiss him goodnight.* Finally she sits by the window and tries to count the stars.

Ross looks at her quizzically when she enters his room at ten. "Two nights in a row, Tiss. To what do I owe this rare treat?" He laughs. "I haven't seen those pajamas in years," he says. He folds back the covers, welcoming her, but instead she sits cross-legged on the bed, facing him and quite close.

"Ross, darling," she says. "You work so hard. I've been thinking that I should try to do the things you ask for. You know, the touching and …"

"Oh, Tiss," he says, his voice husky, "you are full of surprises. This is great. And this is great too." He removes his pajama bottoms and looks her in the eyes.

He loves me so much, she thinks. She tries to move her hand toward his body, but she cannot make it happen. It remains frozen in midair, a few inches above his torso. Her eyes are shut tight. She is thinking of the carousel.

"I know it's hard, my darling Tiss; yes, it's very hard. Here, let me help you." He takes her wrist and guides her hand. She does not resist. He slips off the cotton gloves. "This will warm those cold hands," he says.

Prentiss is riding the painted pony. She grasps the cold metal bar as the pony rises and falls beneath her. She hears the heavy, breathy music of the calliope. The big horse galloping right next to her has flared nostrils and looks fierce. Soon it will froth at the mouth, she knows. It is all very exciting.

"Yes, baby. Yes, yes, yes." Ross is gulping air with each word. His eyes, too, are closed. He does not see her head snap back or hear the tiny shriek. He only feels her hands jerk away, suddenly.

It takes Ross a moment to recover, to realize that Prentiss has fainted. She is lying next to him, her eyes fluttering, softly moaning.

"Oh, my poor darling, Tiss," he says, "too much excitement."

He reaches over and covers her gently. "Here, you can stay with me tonight. You'll be good as new in the morning."

*   *   *   *

When the alarm rings at six, Ross shuts it off with his right hand and with his left gropes for his wife. He smiles as he grasps her thick black hair. More awake now, he can feel that her hair is matted with something warm and sticky. He chuckles softly. He turns on the light and looks at her.

Prentiss' pillow is covered with blood. Her hair and two of her fingers are jammed into her mouth. Her eyes are open but she does not seem to see him. She is humming an inane tune, something old and childlike. He forces her hand from her mouth. One of her fingertips glistens with white bone and sinew; the other is still bleeding.

Ross, trembling, crying, carries his wife to the bathroom. He washes off the blood and wraps her hand in a clean, white towel. He splashes cold water on her face, pleads with her to wake up. "I'll take you to the hospital," he says.

But Prentiss is not asleep. She is at the carousel with Daddy. Soon he will take her for a root beer float. It's going to be a perfect day.

The Grape Fast

I knew I would like them from the moment I opened the door to the waiting room. All four freshly scrubbed and wearing Sunday best. The little girl on Dad's lap turned and buried her face in his chest as soon as she saw me. He tried to rise and extend his hand to me, but the girl whimpered and clung to him. Mom and the older girl, both lean and plain, sat side by side on the sofa. They pulled down the hems of their skirts as I entered. The mother looked up at me and managed a little smile with her mouth. I glanced at her eyes and looked away quickly. Her pain would have to wait. They had come about the little girl.

"This here's Marcie," the man said, and tried to turn her toward me.

I raised a finger and shook my head. "It's okay," I said, "she'll come around later."

In the consultation room, the Marsdens aligned themselves the same way they had in the waiting room. Hank sat in the large rocker with Marcie on his lap. Eloise and Sissy sat next to each other in the walnut ladder-backs. I rolled my swivel chair out from behind the desk and completed the circle.

"Who wants to tell me about this?" I said.

Hank looked at Eloise, but she didn't seem to notice.

Sissy nudged her. "Ma," she whispered.

The mother spoke from a distant place. It was a recitation, a litany of correctly pronounced diagnostic procedures, physicians' names and specialties, and of failed interventions. The others looked down as she spoke. I made notes in the chart. What I really wanted to write was, "This poor little girl has a horrible kind of brain tumor diagnosed and treated by the best specialists in town, and now the family wants me to do something."

"Do your other doctors know that you're coming to see an alternative practitioner?"

I knew that Dr. Levy, the neurosurgeon, wouldn't mind. He might even encourage it as a last-ditch measure. But the other docs would tell them not to waste their money. One of them would probably use the word "quack."

Hank answered. "Doc, we're here because of what you did for the Haggerty boy. They got the place about a half mile from us on Old County Road."

Hank smiled. He reminded me of a big kid, full of hope and enthusiasm.

"Brian's still doing well, is he?" I said.

Hank nodded vigorously.

Yes but, I thought, *the Haggerty boy did not come to me with a fatal illness. True, he had been in a wheelchair, and his hands were so knotted he couldn't feed himself, but he wasn't going to die of it. And he was older. And there was a strong psychological component. And …*

"Helps his dad with the chores before and after school, rides his bike past us everyday. I think he likes Sissy." Hank looked over at his older daughter and raised his eyebrows.

Sissy frowned and stuck out her tongue at him. "'Course he don't play football, but he is on the swim team, ain't he, Sis? Please help us, Doc."

"Hank, Eloise, you do understand that I'm not an expert in brain tumors, right? I'm certainly willing to do what I can, but no promises, okay? Well, except that I can promise that I won't cause Marcie any pain and that my treatments won't have any bad side effects. Now let's have a look at her."

"Sissy, you best help me get Marcie's things off. She don't like it one bit, Doc."

"No, no need for that," I said. "I don't need to examine her in the usual way. I have full confidence in Dr. Levy's assessment. You can leave her clothes on, and she can stay in your lap, Hank."

I turned my attention to Sissy and asked her a few questions about school. In a little while, Marcie turned around and looked at me. I waved my fingers at her and smiled as I continued talking to her sister. Finally Marcie slid down off her dad's lap and went toward the raised sandbox I keep in the corner. She fell twice on her way. Her right hand hung uselessly at her side. Without getting up, I rolled my desk chair over and played in the sand alongside her. I arranged three baby ducks in a row and looked around. "Where's that mommy duck?" I said.

Marcie thrust the plastic mother under my nose and giggled.

"Thank you, Miss Marcie," I said, and looked at her.

A smile skewed the right side of her face. A bit of saliva escaped from the drooping left side of her mouth. The pupil of her left eye was dilated and fixed. Her skin was pale gray, translucent. The two biopsy scars on her hairless skull stared at me. I wanted very badly to look away. I wanted to run home and kiss the glowing face of my own little girl and whisper, "Thank God it's not you."

I left Marcie at the sandbox and sat down again with the Marsdens. "Has the neurosurgeon or the oncologist discussed Marcie's prognosis with you?"

I heard the pompous tone in my voice, the cold, clinical detachment. Before they could answer, I rephrased the question. "I mean, did anyone tell you how long she might live or what to expect?"

Hank glanced over at Marcie. He kept his voice low. "They said they couldn't do no more for her. Just take her home until ... well, when she gets real bad we're supposed to bring her back to the hospital."

"They said forget about Christmas," Sissy said. Her voice was cold, even.

"Now, honey, they didn't say it just that way." Eloise tried to pat her daughter's hand, but Sissy pulled it away sharply.

I had seen plenty of families come apart in the process of trying to deal with the death of a child, especially when they weren't used to talking about awful feelings. I wondered if this was the time to refer them to Marianne. *No,* I thought, *that would be the same as telling them that I, too, expect Marcie to die.* Because of Brian Haggerty, the Marsdens had faith that I could help their child. My own self-doubt could be as poisonous to Marcie as the chemotherapy.

"Okay, folks, here's what we're going to do." I said.

After they left, I made some more notes in Marcie's chart. "Try the grape fast for two weeks: Grapes, preferably black, with seeds. Work up to two pounds per day. Also taught them a hands-on energy healing technique. Do twice a day. Call in ten days or sooner if problems."

Eloise called me right on schedule. She reported that Marcie was eating better, no longer vomiting, and had stopped drooling. Still falling and not using the right hand, but her speech was clearer. I wondered if Eloise could hear the high fives I was snapping in the air.

"Keep up the grapes," I said, "and add some other fresh fruits, nothing else for now. Oh, and the energy healing of course. Call me in another week."

✳   ✳   ✳   ✳

I had never been to North Malone before. It was dark, and the roads were icy, but Hank's directions were excellent. When I arrived, most everyone was gathered around Eloise at the piano, singing Christmas carols. I let myself in and stood uncomfortably at the edge of the crowd, holding the giant stuffed panda behind my back. Finally Hank noticed me. He came over and pumped my hand.

"Hey, Doc. Thanks for coming. You don't know how much it means to us. Let me hang up that coat. You bring a date or is that a present for Marcie?" He laughed like a schoolboy and clapped me on the shoulder a few times.

I tried to apologize for not being able to wrap the panda.

"C'mon, you can give it to her right now," he said.

Hank led me to a small family room behind the kitchen where half a dozen preschoolers, watched over by a bored-looking Sissy, frantically raced from one new toy to another. I didn't know which of the four girls was Marcie. They all had a mop of hair, pretty smiles, and new dresses. But she knew me. She came over and tugged at my jacket. "Mommy says you saved my life. You want to see my new dollhouse Daddy made?"

I held the panda out. It was an inch or so taller than Marcie. She grabbed it, squealing, and ran off to show the others.

"Marcie, what do you say to Dr. Mike?" Hank shouted after her.

"Thank you, Dr. Mike," she said, without turning around.

When most of the guests had gone home and Marcie had gone to bed, Hank sat me down in front of the woodstove and handed me a snifter of applejack brandy.

"Here's to you, Doc," he said, lifting his glass. "Thanks for giving us our Marcie back. And in time for Christmas, too! You're a darn magician." He pulled his chair closer to mine. "Seriously, Doc, do you think it was mostly the diet or mostly the energy healing?"

I shrugged and looked down. The research on energy healing was good, but new. The evidence for the grape fast was mostly anecdotal, from Russia. Intuitively, I felt it was something more. "I think it was your love for Marcie and your faith that she would get well." We were both silent for a moment, then I added, "But let's not take any chances. Let's keep the magic going. Continue the latest diet and keep up the once a day hands-on healing."

*   *   *   *

I was sitting in the consultation room, my feet propped up on the desk, and looking out the window at the new buds on the row of linden trees in Lincoln Square. The phone rang, but I let the machine take it. I wanted to finish my lunch, for once, before the afternoon patients arrived. I heard Eloise Marsden's voice, her tone urgent. I snatched up the receiver.

"Eloise, yes, I'm here. What's wrong?"

"It's Marcie, Doctor," Eloise said. "She woke up crying about her head, then started vomiting. She can't stop. She's getting really weak."

A giant's fist was squeezing the breath out of me. I hoped Eloise couldn't hear it. I faked a calm, professional tone.

"It's probably just a stomach virus," I said. "Kids get that kind of thing all the time. But with her past history, I think you should take her to the Pediatric ER at Saint Mary's. I'll alert the house staff."

If my afternoon patients found me abrupt and preoccupied, they didn't say. After the last one, I ran the six blocks to the hospital. The charge nurse informed me that Marcie was still in the ER and pointed to the third cubicle. I hadn't taken more than three steps in that direction when I saw Dr. Levy and a neurosurgical resident emerge from the exam room. I stood there, very still, my palms together, as he approached.

"It's come back, Mike—with a vengeance," he said, laying a hand on my shoulder. "Whatever miracle you wrought is no longer working. We'll admit her, of course, to relieve the pressure, but there's not much else we can do. They really want to see you."

I stayed with the family the rest of the night and into the next day, meditating and praying with them at Marcie's bedside. By late that afternoon she went into a coma from which she never recovered.

After the funeral, Hank asked me to come over to the house for awhile. He said that he and Eloise wanted to thank me. They still considered it miraculous that Marcie had come back to normal and was with them for Christmas and into the spring.

I just nodded. I couldn't think of anything to say, because I felt like I didn't know anything. I really didn't know what it was that had helped Marcie to heal and I certainly didn't know why the tumor had recurred.

I told Hank and Eloise that I would stay in touch and let myself out of the house while they were occupied with other friends and relatives. As I was walking to my car, Sissy came up behind me.

"Dr. Mike, can I ask you something?"

"Sure, Sissy."

"Do you think it made any difference, I mean, Dad stopped doing that healing thing with Marcie a few weeks ago. Me and Mom still did it every morning even though Marcie laughed through most of it. I was just thinking …"

"Why did your dad stop?" I was trying to sound curious, not accusatory. I knew how close Hank and Marcie had been.

"Oh, he didn't *want* to stop. It's just that they changed his shift at the plant and he couldn't be around in the morning, and me and Mom, we were too busy to do it later when Dad came home. We thought that two of us, in the morning like always, would be okay. So do you think it made any difference?"

I stood silently for a few moments, looking up at the weathervane on the garage roof. I was hoping Sissy would think I needed time to consider the answer to her question. I hoped she wouldn't know I was lying to her.

"No, Sis, I'm sure it didn't."

Grandpa Zake

When we were first given the assignment to write a short memoir about someone, other than our parents, who had had a real impact on our lives, I couldn't think of anyone. My roommate suggested a certain instructor, because she knows I always get weak in the knees when I see him, but I told her I didn't think that was the kind of impact Professor Knoble had in mind. Then she started talking about some of the boys we know here at college who are kind of different, and that made me think of my Grandpa Zake.

Most of my friends make fun of these guys and wouldn't consider dating them. I pretend to agree with my friends, but I have to admit that I find some of these men fascinating. I'm drawn to them just like I was to Grandpa Zake when I was a kid. If a guy like that is gay, then I just think of him as a normal gay man, and I can be his friend. But if he's not gay, and he starts acting like he's interested in going out with me ... well, I suddenly become very busy. But let me get back to Grandpa Zake.

When I was little, the first thing he did when he came to our house was to shut off the TV. "Bad for your mind, bad for your eyes, bad for your soul," he'd say, even though my mom explained to him that we could only watch two hours a day and that it was all PBS and the Discovery channel. Then he would take us outside and parade us around the yard and sing something about marching to Praetoria, or "Hup, two, three, four. Hup, two, three, four. I know a kid, her name is Sue (me), prettiest gal I ever knew. Hup, two, three, four." And we'd get into it, my little brothers and I, marching around the yard behind Grandpa Zake and singing and banging on tin cans. We didn't know enough then to care about what the neighbors thought, especially the old lady next door peering out through a crack in the venetian blinds.

Then we would stand facing the sun and do breathing exercises. Grandpa Zake called it "chee-kung," explaining that he learned the exercises from an old Chinese man. He told us that the ancient Taoists had secrets that were the key to health and a long life. I didn't know what he was talking about back then, but he was so enthusiastic, it was contagious. I even tried to teach the exercises to some of my friends, but they would get me laughing, and that would be the end of it.

When I got older, of course, I learned facts in school and from TV science shows, and then I wouldn't have anything to do with Grandpa Zake's silly exercises. I didn't want to hurt his feelings, so I would just tell him that I had too much homework or had a headache or something. And now, being premed, I sometimes argue with him. That is, I *try* to argue with him, but he just smiles and says, "You are learning so much, Suzie Sunshine."

And that's what some of those guys I know are like. For instance, one time I walked into Justin's dorm room and found him meditating on a cushion on the floor. He smiled up at me in such a sweet way and offered me a cushion. I sort of wanted to give it a try, but then I thought what if one of my friends walked in, so I flashed him a give-me-a-break look and left. Another time I was walking back to the dorm after French class with Justin, and he out of the blue said to me, "You don't need to be afraid to look inside yourself, you know. I can tell from your eyes that you won't find anything bad in there."

I saw him standing there just looking at me in a way that made me feel like I'd known him all my life. I knew I wanted to hug him then, but I also knew that if I did, I would start crying. So I looked at my watch instead and said something mean like I had to get back because

Brett was picking me up in a half hour. Justin didn't know that the only interest Brett had in me was to help him get through biochem.

Grandpa Zake took me to my first Broadway show. It was a revival of *Oklahoma!* put on by a New York City company on tour. On the way back home in the car, he taught me to sing,

> Chicks and ducks and geese better scurry
> When I take you out in the surrey,
> When I take you out in the surrey
> With the fringe … on top.

And all the rest of the lyrics to that tune, which I still remember. I went around the house for days singing that silly song and making hoofbeat sounds with my tongue. He also took me to my first ballet performance, and afterward in the parking lot, taught me to do a pirouette. I took ballet lessons for about seven years after that—which Grandpa Zake paid for. He always came to my recitals with my mom; my dad was always too busy. One time one of the other girls asked if that was my dad, and when I sarcastically replied how could she think that old fart could be my father, she said, "I don't think he looks old at all. I think he looks like Hugh Grant." Which I guess he sort of does, only taller, and with gray hair.

My brothers used to complain that Grandpa Zake never came to any of their things, like Little League games or hockey. One day I overheard my mom in the kitchen with him. He was preparing a soufflé and mom was suggesting that he make an effort to go to Matt's and Brian's games once in a while. I could hear that he stopped whisking.

He said, "Anna dear, I thought you knew me better than that." It almost sounded like he was crying. Then he said, "Oh, shit, I've ruined the batter."

That reminds me that one time a couple of years ago, I went with Justin over to his friend Dalton's apartment one Sunday morning. We were going to learn to make French omelets, I guess, because Professor Robillard had been talking in class (in French of course) about how there is nothing that compares to the way eggs are prepared in France. I had never even boiled an egg, so I got to observe while Dalton taught Justin the fine points: using a copper bowl to whisk, lightly; pouring the egg at just the right time into the pan which had to be at just the right temperature (you could tell from the color and the aroma of the butter, if you were experienced); and then, hardest of all, the subtle movements of the pan and the spatula while the egg cooked, fast. And then sliding the bubbly, lightly browned omelet on to a preheated plate. This one Dalton gave to me, with the admonition to "never, no never, have toast with a French omelet." A bit of cheese perhaps, and afterward, a *petit pain* with fresh butter and *café au lait*. It was the best egg I'd ever tasted, and I wished Grandpa Zake had been there so I could have teased him about his being too greasy.

Then Dalton went out to meet his friend in Riverside Park, leaving me alone with Justin in the apartment. Justin put on a CD of Mahler's *Fourth*, which happens to be one of my favorites, and made me sit in the sun in the breakfast nook where I could look out and see the river. I sat watching him do the dishes and clean the counters, all the while feeling the sun on my legs. I was dying to ask him if Dalton was gay and, of course, what was their relationship, when all of a sudden he half turned to me with a dishtowel draped over his shoulder and said, "Dalton is gay, in case you're wondering—he's meeting Evan in the park."

At this point, he twirled in a nearly perfect pirouette, swinging the dishtowel wildly overhead, and sent it flying in my direction. It landed on my head, covering my face. I protested with a laugh and tossed it back at him.

"Mahler is so great," he said, walking toward me, "and so are you, Suzanne in the Sunshine." He took the towel from my hands and smoothed my hair back into place and kissed me lightly on the cheek.

I remember I looked up into his clear, kind eyes, so close to mine. "I'm feeling a bit dizzy," I said. "It must be the Bloody Mary."

Justin took both my hands in his and looked into my face. "Suzy, I'm not gay. I'm just not like most of the other straight guys."

The dizziness went away, but then I felt like someone had grabbed my heart in his fist and was squeezing it. I asked him if we could take a walk in the park. He smiled and went into the living room to get my sweater.

*   *   *   *

When I was about sixteen, my Grandma Helen, Grandpa Zake's second wife, became ill with lung cancer. She had the usual treatments, and they helped for awhile, but she kept getting recurrences. Then Grandpa Zake took her to all kinds of alternative doctors and clinics, including some in Switzerland and one in Nepal, but nothing seemed to make much difference. After about a year of this, she stayed in bed waiting to die. Grandpa Zake finally hired a nurse's aide to come in once in a while so he could get a break from the routine.

He came over to our house a lot for dinner, which he usually wound up making from items he'd gotten at the natural foods store. I remember a lot of stir-fries with tofu and mushrooms and unidentifiable greens that Mom and I really liked. After dinner, Dad usually took the boys out somewhere, I suspect to MacDonald's, and Mom and Grandpa Zake and I did the dishes and sang old songs he had taught us.

One Saturday night, David, my sort of boyfriend at the time, took me out to Pasha's for dinner. He was older and had a night license and could drink legally. He ordered a Jose Cuervo on the rocks and gave me a sip. It went down the wrong way, and I started coughing and hiccupping. David apparently thought this was funny and started laughing at me. I got pissed off and ran to the bar for some water. It was then that I saw Grandpa Zake. He was sitting only about three stools away, but his back was to me, because he had turned to face some pretty woman on the next stool. He was touching her face with his left hand, and their heads were very close together. It was really noisy in the bar, but I could tell he was singing something to her. I caught enough of it to know it was one of his favorites, one that he had taught to me the time he had taken me to see an old Walter Houston film.

> Oh, it's a long, long time
> From May to December,
> And the days grow short
> When you reach September.
>
> And the autumn weather
> Turns the leaves to flame,
> And one hasn't got time
> For the waiting game.

I left the bar before he got to the part about "these few precious days I'll spend with you."

I went back to the table and told David I wasn't feeling well and wanted him to take me home. He tried to kiss me and touch my breast before he let me out of the car, but I told him, "Get out of here—you're drunk," which he wasn't. I just had to get away by myself so I could think.

It took me a long time to get over being mad at Grandpa Zake. I acted sullen around him, especially after Grandma Helen died, but I never said anything to him about seeing him in the bar. I'm still not sure I forgive him.

∗   ∗   ∗   ∗

I turned twenty during exam week last semester, so there was no chance of going home to my parents. They called and wished me a happy birthday, and even my brothers got on the phone. Grandpa Zake sent me a dozen pink roses with a silly poem attached, addressed as usual to Suzie Sunshine.

Justin and I were studying together for the French 403 exam when the roses came. He insisted that I let him take me out to dinner in spite of all the studying we had to do. "Twenty is big," he said, slamming the book on Baudelaire and getting my down jacket off the bed. "We can walk to Sarabeth's Kitchen, have a healthy feast, and come right back to the books."

While we were waiting for the food, Justin started drumming on the table with the chopsticks he always carried and singing "Happy Birthday" in French, sotto voce, so I wouldn't get embarrassed. Then he leaned over and whispered, "Happy birthday, Suzie Sunshine," in my ear. He started to give me a kiss on the cheek, but I turned my head and kissed him full on the mouth. He looked into my eyes and smiled that sweet smile of his and said, "I love you, Sue."

"I know," I said. And then the food arrived.

To Charlie the Swimmer Boy, with Love from Mona

The summer I turned twelve, my mom finally let me go over to Joannie and Barb's cottage when they went swimming. Poor Mom. I picture her back at our place trying to concentrate on a novel but getting up every two minutes to look down the road to see if I was on my way home and not dead at the bottom of the lake.

Usually, my mom was fun to be with. She danced with me while we made dinner. One time she taught me the tango, a wooden spoon clenched between her teeth. In the car, when Dad wasn't with us, she drove fast, whipping through yellow lights without slowing down, singing. And she made her friends laugh a lot with what they called her "double entendres," most of which I didn't get.

But get her around water and she stopped breathing. Even the bathtub. She used to sit right next to the old claw-foot while I took my bath, and when I dunked under to rinse my hair, she hung over the tub, her hand poised in rescue mode. So I was really surprised when she and Dad bought the cottage.

We started spending summers at the lake when I was seven. "Aunt" Gert and "Uncle" Phil Merkins, Joannie and Barb's parents, had the cottage next door, and the girls and I were together a lot, but never around the water. We went bike riding on nice days and played Monopoly on their porch when it rained. I was glad that they never even asked me about swimming. I didn't figure out until years later that Mom must have gotten to them.

When it was really hot, Mom would go "bathing" in the lake and she took me with her. We both wore white rubber caps on our heads and white rubber slippers on our feet and black woolen bathing suits. She held on to the dock with one hand and walked out until the water reached the hem of her suit. Then she would cup a few teaspoons in her hand and splash it over her shoulders and back, drawing her breath in sharply and shivering. "Oooh," she would say. When she was finished she would let me dunk down in the water while she held my hand.

When my dad came out to the cottage after work, he would always go for a "dip" before dinner. I wanted to go in the water with him, but Mom wouldn't hear of it. I only remember them arguing about it one time. It ended when Mom reminded him about her once having had an older brother and about the well on Grandpa's farm.

I went down to the lake with Dad and watched from the dock. He strode quickly into the chilly blue water, held his nose and slipped below the surface. He lay there in the dead man's float much longer, I thought, than a normal human being could. Then he surfaced with a mighty, "Aaaah," and reached for his towel and glasses.

When I got to be twelve, Mom stopped making me wear the rubber cap and slippers, and Dad bought me a real Dacron bathing suit. I still couldn't swim, but that's when Mom started letting me go over to the Merkins'. One day Joannie came over and knocked on the screen door to the porch where I was reading. *All Dogs Go to Heaven*, I think it was.

"Charlie," she said, "Barb says if you want to come over, you have to bring the new tube your dad got for you."

"Fine," I said, "but you have to help carry it." One of Dad's patients had given him a tube from the rear tire of his John Deere in lieu of payment. The thing was a monster. I figured you could float all the way to England in it. Joannie and I took it over to the Merkins' and launched it off the end of the dock. Joannie and Barb dove in after the tube and surfaced together inside its perimeter, sputtering and giggling. Then they swam out to the float to work on their tans.

Uncle Phil had used old barrels and scrap lumber to build the float, which he anchored fifty feet off the end of the dock. He was handy with his hands that way, even though my dad was a lot smarter. My mom, too, seemed to know a lot more about books and music than Aunt Gert did. Joannie was in my class, and it seemed like I was always helping her with her homework. Barb was already in high school and did okay, but she was taking mostly business courses. On the other hand, the girls could swim and I couldn't. There are a lot of different ways of being smart, and I wasn't sure ours was the best.

Out on the float, Barb looked around and then pulled the top of her bathing suit down. I pretended not to watch, and I think she pretended I couldn't see that far. Or maybe she thought I was too young to be interested. While I was looking and not looking, the tube started drifting away from the dock. I didn't notice it until it was too late for me to retrieve it.

"Joannie, Barb!" I yelled. "The tube's getting away."

"Jesus, Charlie, what a pest you are," Joannie said.

She rolled into the water, swam to the escaping tube, and hauled it back to the dock. "Get in, Chuck-o," she said. "I'll give you a ride out to the float."

My mom's water caution flooded my mind, but only for a moment. I was thinking about something else. I only hoped Barb wouldn't pull up her top before I got there.

*   *   *   *

That evening at dinner, Mom looked across the table at Dad in a way I'd seen before. She had her chin tucked in, and she was peering out at him from under her eyebrows. It meant she was preparing to tell him something he did not want to hear.

"Joey, dear," she said, "my brother Abe called. He's driving up from the City tomorrow. He wants to try out the new Packard and …"

"Don't I work hard enough all week? I should have to put up with his mooching on the weekend? And … and what?" my dad said. He took off his glasses and stared at Mom. I think he already knew but wanted to make her say it.

"Well, he's bringing his new girlfriend. He says they're almost engaged."

"Almost engaged." Dad grinned and winked at me. "We've heard that one before, haven't we, Charlie. Every year a new car and a new girlfriend. Another shiksa bites the dust."

I shrugged and nodded and raised my palms. "What can you do?" it meant.

*   *   *   *

I was sitting on the back porch steps chopping walnuts for Mom's kuchen and watching for the Packard convertible. I'd never seen one. Uncle Abe always had great new cars. A couple of years before, he'd come up in a LaSalle roadster with a rumble seat in the back, and he'd taken me and Joannie around the lake in it. We put on goggles and pretended we were World War I pilots. Last year he had a Willys Overland which he let me steer while he worked the pedals. Mom and Dad were in the backseat, Mom laughing and yelling. Dad sat very still, except for his eyes, which I could see in the rearview mirror. They were jumping back and forth between the lake and the road.

I had to agree with my dad that Uncle Abe wasn't too smart. Similar to Uncle Phil, except that he wasn't good at building things. But he was great at sports. The only five-star athlete in his high school, he always said. He had the yearbook to prove it, so Dad couldn't even raise an eyebrow. And he always brought me neat stuff in boxes that said Spaulding Official this or that. He tried to teach me to use it, but when he went back to the city, I didn't have anyone to practice with, so the stuff collected dust on the closet shelves.

And it's true what my dad said about Uncle Abe's girlfriends. They were dumb blondes. And they were freeloaders, which was hard on Mom. They'd sleep until noon, soak up the sun, drink all the rum and coke in the house. They'd just pick at the meals my mom had worked so hard to fix and never offer to help with the dishes. And about the third day, they started with the whine. "Abe, honey, I miss New Yawk. When are we going back?" I couldn't see any way that they were smart.

When the Packard pulled into the gravel driveway, the late afternoon sun bounced off the windshield and right into my eyes. I stood up too fast and spilled half the walnuts on the steps. I jumped off the porch and started sort of sauntering toward the car, trying to look casual and grown-up.

Uncle Abe climbed out of the driver's side. He stood on the running board in his houndstooth knickers and matching cap and surveyed the countryside.

"Hi, Uncle Abe," I said.

"Hey, kid, how's it goin'?" He tossed me the car keys. "Do me a favor. Get my clubs and both suitcases out of the trunk. But don't touch the Speed Graphic. It's brand new. Wait'll you see what it can do."

The leather suitcases were pretty heavy, and I had to crawl halfway into the trunk to reach the golf clubs. While I was in there, I could hear Uncle Abe talking to his girlfriend.

"Listen, Mona, the kid's name is Charlie, my sister is Vera, and my brother-in-law is Joey—try and get it right."

This one must be even less smart than the others, I thought.

I closed the trunk lid and peered through the bouquet of woods and irons which I was attempting to hoist onto my shoulder. Mona emerged from the leather cocoon of the Packard's front seat, slowly, like she'd been asleep, or like she was visiting another planet. Her feet, in red and white open-toe platform heels with matching red polish on her toenails, seemed to be testing the uneven gravel of the driveway. She stood up on her tan legs, which seemed to go on forever. She was wearing short white shorts and a white halter top, both edged in the same red, and she had a red ribbon in her blonde hair. She turned toward me. I tried to look real busy with the golf clubs.

"Hi, Cholly. Pleased ta meetcha."

I wasn't sure I could talk. "Me too," I said. It sounded kind of squeaky. Luckily, my mom came out through the screen door at that moment and rushed toward Uncle Abe with her welcoming arms. She was wearing an apron, and there was a smudge of pastry flour on her cheek.

"Abela, Abela. Such a long time," she said, hugging him. She turned toward Mona, smiling and extending both hands. "And this must be …"

"Pleased ta meetcha, Vera."

"Vee, this is Mona," said Uncle Abe. "Isn't she a doll? You should see her dance!"

*   *   *   *

My dad arrived home as Mom was pouring the second round of whiskey sours. He sniffed the air and frowned. "What's that you're drinking, young man?" he said.

"It's okay, Dad. It's a Wispy Sour. Mona learned to make them from the bartender at the Copa, didn't you, Mona? It tastes just like the real thing. I mean, I think it tastes just like the real thing. Wanna taste it? Mona's gonna show me how so I can make them for Joannie and Barb."

My dad flashed his work smile at Mona. "I'm Joseph, as you must have surmised. My son seems quite taken with you. If you'll excuse me, I'll wash up for dinner. Hello, Abe. Nice car."

"Pleased ta meetcha, Joey," said Mona.

Dad turned toward the stairs. "Oh, Charlie, put Uncle Abe's bag up in the guest room, as usual. And Mona's you can put on the screened-in porch, next to the pullout sofa." He nodded meaningfully at my mom.

I woke up earlier than usual the next morning. I think it was Uncle Abe's loud voice from the kitchen, talking to my mom. He was telling her to hurry up with his breakfast because he had to get out on the links while it was still cool. He bossed Mom around more than my dad ever did, but she didn't seem to mind, even though he was her kid brother.

On my way to the bathroom, I passed by the guest room door and saw Uncle Abe's suitcase lying open on the floor. I went in to look for the Spaulding box.

"G'mawning, Chollie, nice pj's you got. Now I know what to bring ya the next time I come up."

I froze in my tracks. I felt like a burglar caught sneaking around in someone's house. I looked down at my Fruit of the Loom briefs, then grinned sheepishly at Mona. I wanted to tell her that I had lots of pajamas and that I just couldn't be bothered to put them on last night. I wanted to ask her what she was doing here since I thought she was asleep downstairs on the porch. But I couldn't tell her anything. I couldn't even breathe.

Mona was sitting up in bed, leaning back against the headboard, naked. She turned toward the nightstand and reached for a cigarette. I figured I should run out, but I couldn't even move. I figured I shouldn't keep looking, but I couldn't not look. Besides, her breasts were everywhere. Everywhere my eyes went—her hair, the pack of cigarettes in her hand, the box of matches—there were Mona's breasts.

My heart was beating so fast I thought I would pass out. And I had to pee so bad it made me nauseous. And then there was this other problem. I could feel it pushing against my underpants like some live animal that wanted to get loose. I was afraid to look down, and I was more afraid that Mona would look down. But not to look down meant continuing to look at her breasts, which were still everywhere. Somehow I had to get out of there.

When Mona lit her cigarette, I said, "Do you always smoke Luckies?" I pointed to the red and white pack on the nightstand. Mona turned to look at the cigarettes. "So does my Mom ... smoke Luckies," I said. "You two have some things in common. Well, I have to go, it's really getting late. See you later." I escaped into the bathroom.

Downstairs in the kitchen, Uncle Abe had gone and my mom was up to her elbows in dirty dishwater. I could hear my dad outside mowing the lawn.

"Oh, there you are, honey," Mom said, brushing strands of loose hair from her face with the back of her wrist. "Can you get your own breakfast, please, dear? I need to finish the dishes and start on lunch. Uncle Abe will be back from the course in a few hours, and you know how he loves a big lunch after golf. Oh, and Charlie ..."

Mom dried her hands and steered me out onto the front porch where the unused sofa bed seemed to be mocking me. She spoke in a whisper. "Honey, can you keep Mona occupied for an hour or two while I get some work done? Try and get her out of the cottage. A walk down the old road or over to the Merkins' or ..."

"I'll think of something, Ma, don't worry. I'll start by making her breakfast. If she ever comes down, that is." I glanced toward the stairs.

Mona walked into the kitchen a few minutes later. It looked to me like she had plans of her own. She was wearing a two-piece red bathing suit and a pair of horn-rimmed sunglasses. She carried a rolled-up towel and a bottle of Coppertone. I peered intently into the half-open door of the icebox. "What would you like for breakfast?" I asked.

"Yer a sweet kid, Cholly. Have you got a Coke in there?" she said. "Listen, I got to work on my tan. Why don'tcha put on yer bathing suit and keep me company."

*   *   *   *

I led Mona down the front hill and across the road to the splintery staircase that went down to the dock. Mona stood in the shimmering August heat and slowly stretched her arms toward the sun, her palms facing each other. It looked like she was reaching for something that she could see and I couldn't. Then, without a word, she bounded to the end of the dock and dove into the still, blue lake. Her body seemed to slice the water like a knife. She hardly made a ripple. When she came to the surface, she turned and smiled up at me. "C'mon in, Cholly—the water's fine."

I sat down at the end of the dock, busying myself with a loose board. Mona swam over and stood in the waist-deep water. She put an icy hand on my knee and looked right into my eyes. "Ya can't swim, can ya, Cholly?"

She said this very softly, like it really mattered to her and like she knew it really mattered to me. I shook my head and inspected the loose board more closely.

"C'mon," Mona said. "It's gonna be alright."

She took both my hands and slid me into the water. I gasped in spite of myself and squeezed her hands tightly. Mona leaned down and spoke close to my face. "I'm gonna teach ya to swim, and yer not gonna drown, okay?"

"Okay," I said, and I knew it *would* be okay.

Mona held me while I floated on my back and then on my belly like my dad in the dead man's float. She told me to nod my head when I felt it would be safe for her to let go of me. I gave her the signal. There I was, floating by myself, like magic, like flying, I thought. Then she taught me the doggie paddle, which was easy, and then she taught me how to do the Australian crawl, like she did. It was all okay. Within a half hour we were swimming circles off the end of the dock. Me and Mona, swimming together.

Finally we stood in the water at the side of the dock. Mona put her arms around me and held me to her chest. "Yer a great kid, Cholly."

I wanted to hug her back but I was afraid I would never be able to let go.

"Gee, thanks," I said.

✳   ✳   ✳   ✳

After dinner that evening, the adults played canasta on the screened-in porch. I sat on a stool next to Mona, very close, so she could teach me the game. I tried hard to pay attention, but the soft, yellow light from the lamp and the dull thudding of insects against the screen and the dreamy scent of Mona's suntan lotion made me sleepy. My head kept nodding, and my feet kept slipping off the rung of the stool. When Dad insisted that I go up to bed, I protested, but was secretly relieved.

The next morning when I came down to breakfast, Mom and Dad were at the kitchen table drinking coffee. They were whispering about something and snickering.

"Where's Uncle Abe and Mona?" I asked.

"They had to get an early start back to the city, dear. Mona has an audition tonight at the Latin Quarter," my mom said, grinning at my dad, who snorted and seemed to be trying not to laugh.

"She ... they didn't even say good-bye," I said.

"Well, you didn't miss much, in my opinion," Dad said. "She could hardly put one word in front of the other. A genius she was not. Right, Charlie?"

I looked down at my feet. "I guess not," I said.

"She did leave this for you, dear."

Mom handed me an envelope. It said: "To Charlie the Swimmer Boy with Love from Mona." Inside was a black-and-white photograph with sawtooth edges. It was a picture of Mona in a bathing suit standing near a palm tree with a sandy beach and the ocean in the background. She is smiling and waving at the camera.

When the Student
Is Ready

When David arrived that snowy Sunday morning, several of the others were already there, seated on floor cushions or folded blankets. He chose a straight-backed chair by the door, the lotus—or even half of that—no longer suited to his old bones. David could smell Tess' cinnamon-apple streusel baking in the oven and fresh ground coffee perking on the stovetop. He nodded to the others, then centered himself, closed his eyes, and focused on his breath, waiting for Bill to signal the start of the meditation.

The door opened, and at first he thought it was the wind, as he had heard no footsteps. He looked up to see a young woman, standing, smiling, a little unsure of herself. She took off her woolen scarf and tossed her head, sending an avalanche of freshly washed blonde waves down her shoulders. The scent of her shampoo and a few snowflakes landed on his face, like moist kisses. David's breath forgot itself.

Bill walked over to her with open arms, beaming a welcome. The young woman hugged Bill and kissed him on the cheek. Tess, Bill's wife, a thin, graying brunette, stood tentatively beside him.

"Hey, everybody," said Bill, "this is Cassie. Cassie, meet David, Maureen, Sally, Alex, Sandor, Aviva, and my wife, Tess. There are six more of us, but some are out of town, and others hate snow."

David stood and extended his hand to Cassie. She took it in both of hers, looked deeply into his eyes and smiled. For a moment, there was no one else in the room. As David watched her greet each of the others in the same manner, his shoulders sagged and his breath returned.

Aviva insisted on giving Cassie a long, full-body hug. David was annoyed and resolved, again, that one of these days he was going to ask Aviva if she was aware that some people might not want that. He had been putting it off, dreading the nodding, knowing smile and the spiritual doublespeak she would offer in return.

After everyone was seated, Tess opened the Jack Kornfield book to a page she had dog-eared. Bill held up his hand and turned to Cassie.

"Cassie told me that she would like to share with you a little about why she's here. So before we start the reading and the sitting ..." Bill opened his palm and smiled at Cassie. David thought he recognized Bill's "you poor dear" smile, the same smile he had seen Bill extend to Melanie, David's wife, who had died the year before of brain cancer. Bill was an oncologist, a damn fine one, as David knew. And a very compassionate fellow.

Cassie sat straight on her cushion, like a ballerina, and lengthened her neck gracefully. She glanced around the room, her face flushed, her green eyes misty and sorrowful. Yet she smiled as she spoke, and a gentle, lilting laugh punctuated most of her sentences. David wondered if he would ever see her without the smile. He thought she might be even more beautiful.

"Bill is such a dear," said Cassie. "He would never reveal that I am one of his patients. I have breast cancer." Cassie cupped her right hand in front of her left breast, then let it settle in her lap again. "I've had a lumpectomy, but I refused radiation. There are a few nodes, up here, under the arm, so Bill wants me to have chemo, of course. I've been through that before. It's a long story, which I won't go into now, but well, I can't face it again. I'm here because I believe meditation will be helpful to me. And of course the support. Spiritual support and guidance, but not the churchy kind, you know. Bill says you people are just great."

Cassie lowered her eyes and smoothed her skirt over the cushion.

David looked around the room. Some of the others had tears in their eyes, some looked away. Aviva continued nodding and smiling. David sighed, aware that his thoughts had taken a cynical turn. The previous week's readings had focused on "gifts," on how everything that comes our way should be seen as an opportunity for growth. Cassie's cancer a gift to her? Bullshit. David did his best to dispel the negative thoughts, but then he couldn't remember if he was supposed to shut the thoughts out or focus on them until they faded. Two years of weekly readings and sittings, and he was still a beginner.

Tess read a few paragraphs from Kornfield. Bill tapped the brass singing bowl with a soft mallet, signaling the start of the meditation.

During the social hour, several people clustered around Cassie. David took his cake and coffee across the room and sat down near the front window next to Alex, both of them facing the blizzard. They talked about snowblowers and firewood.

∗   ∗   ∗   ∗

The first Sunday in April was warm enough for the group to meet outdoors on Maureen's deck. The sound of the creek, as it rushed and tumbled over shale and pebbles, almost drowned out the whine of traffic from the overpass. The sun was bright and hot by midmorning, when they assembled. Most of the group wore shorts and T-shirts. Alex, shirtless, was stretched out on the chaise, laughing and telling the group he could tan and meditate simultaneously.

David had turned his back to the sun and pulled his cap low over his eyes. He had hoped they would meet in Maureen's comfortable family room, but kept his mouth shut, unwilling to be the spoilsport. He was already feeling annoyed by the buzzing of gnats in his ears and the rivulets of sweat tickling his neck. Do not curse the distractions, he told himself, recalling the readings. The distractions are not the enemy. It is you who choose to struggle with them rather than to open yourself to the song within. *Or something like that*, he thought.

Cassie wore Mexican sandals and a jade ankle bracelet. She had on a gauzy, filmy, earth-toned dress that swished when she moved. To David, she appeared to have lost some weight, but her smile was as bright as ever. She told the group before the sitting that there were some spots on her lungs, but that she was still resistant to Bill's recommendations for chemotherapy.

"I know I should," she said, "but my angels are telling me that my healing lies elsewhere." She laughed her musical laugh.

After the sitting, David walked with her over to the edge of the creek. They both held glasses of Maureen's iced Banja tea.

"Tell me about what the angels are saying to you," David said.

Cassie held the glass to her lips and looked up at David. "They don't really talk to me in words, David, so don't go making any diagnoses. I just get these images."

David wondered who had told Cassie that he was a psychiatrist. He hoped she wouldn't think he was being cynical, because, right now, he wasn't.

"No, really, Cassie. I want to hear about this."

"Sometimes when I meditate, but more often when I'm dropping off to sleep, I see swirling blue water laced with golden sunshine, and, at the same time, I feel a surge of energy through my body, a vibrancy. Like pure health, or something," Cassie laughed and did a pirouette in the grass.

David smiled. "A vacation in Bali, maybe?"

"Is that an invitation?" Cassie laughed again and punched David's shoulder. "Just kidding. But hey, Bali couldn't hurt, if Devon and I could afford it. But no, I see other things as well. Heaps of colorful fruits and vegetables. Thin, silvery needles, quivering. Oh, and hands, warm, strong hands on my body."

"Cassie, you're describing a health spa. Whirlpool baths, healthy diet, massage. And acupuncture too, I would guess. Sounds great. Go for it."

Cassie took a step closer to David and lowered her voice. Her gaze was direct and serious, but she never stopped smiling. "That's what Devon said when I told him about the images. Poor guy. He'd like nothing better than to take me to a place like that. But he knows he can't, and it makes him feel awful."

David flushed. Cassie was the kind of woman who brings out rescue fantasies in men. David longed to reach into his pocket and write out a check to Canyon Ranch. Let her fill in the amount when she was healed. He knew, of course, that he couldn't do that. He felt frustrated, not knowing what to say. Cassie's angels were right. If that's what she believed in, it would help, maybe cure. Money shouldn't stand in the way. *If only* Melanie *had been willing,* he thought.

"Shit," he said. "Our fucking health care system. They'll pay millions for poisonous drugs and mutilating surgery, but not a penny for gentle, natural healing. The Europeans? They go to the spas and the government picks up the tab. Pisses me off."

Cassie put her hand on David's arm. "Hey, David, it's not your problem. But you are very sweet. Maybe something will come along. I've got to trust in the angels."

A crazy idea popped into David's mind. *Maybe it's not so crazy,* he thought. *Trust your intuition.* He decided to risk sounding like a fool. He took both of Cassie's hands in his own and spoke urgently.

"Cassie, look. This group, the people who sit together on Sundays? We're committed to service as a way of life. Not acts of self-abasement, but a caring for others in whatever way we can. I'd like your permission to bring it up with them. Your dilemma, I mean."

Cassie hesitated. Her smile seemed as if it might fade, then shone brightly again. "Well, sure. Hey, why not?"

"Good," said David. They started back toward the group on the deck. "Cassie, why angels? Why isn't it just your intuition guiding you?"

"You don't believe in angels?" she said.

*   *   *   *

A month later, the group held a benefit party for Cassie at the Come Back Inn. The PR committee had done a great job; over two hundred people attended. Sally's band played, David recited a few of his poems, Alex juggled and told jokes. Cassie herself sang and danced to a recording of "I Could Have Danced All Night." The rest of the crew served food they had made and offered booze at an inflated price. They raised seven thousand dollars.

David sat at a table with Alex, Maureen, Cassie, and Devon, Cassie's husband. David thought Devon looked very young, like an overgrown kid. He seemed to stick pretty close to Cassie and didn't say much. When Cassie was performing, Devon gazed at her, starry-eyed, his mouth open. As David watched Cassie, an image came to him: a little girl dressed in tights and a tutu, dancing and singing her heart out for her parents, and smiling, smiling, smiling.

When Cassie returned to the table, David said, "Cassie, you were great. I had no idea you were so talented. Have you done musical theatre?"

"Oh, well, does almost count?" Cassie laughed her musical laugh. "Before I met Devon, I was a student at SUNY-Purchase. Performing Arts. I'd been singing and acting since I was a little kid. In my senior year I was diagnosed with osteogenic sarcoma. My parents took me to Roswell Park. I had chemo, the whole nine yards. I was sick as a dog, lost all my hair. I hated it, but I was cured. But not in time to finish school that year. I went to work in a day care center for preschoolers. That's where I met Devon."

"I wasn't one of the kids," said Devon, grinning. "I was an aide."

"Anyway," said Cassie, "the rest is history. We've been together ever since." Cassie reached across the table and patted Devon's arm. A "Good dog" pat, thought David.

"You never went back to performing?" Maureen said.

"I … we had to earn a living. Did you know I run a children's performing arts center?"

"Now, you mean?"

"Yes, for the past twenty years. Cassie's Sunshine Center."

"Everybody loves her," said Devon. "The kids, the parents. They'd never let her quit, right, honey?"

David put down his fork and pushed away his plate of half-eaten quiche. He took a sip of coffee, which tasted bitter in his mouth. Do not judge the path of another, he told himself.

*   *   *   *

When Cassie returned from the spa, she looked radiant. She told the group that she hadn't felt that good in years.

Someone said, "I bet you wish you could stay there forever."

Cassie made a sharp intake of breath, then laughed. "I feel great," she said. "I can't wait to get back to work."

Bill clapped his hands. "I have to tell you," he said, pointing to himself. "The doctor was wrong. The patient knew what she needed. Cassie's chest films are clear, totally free of tumor." The group applauded, stomped, and whistled.

Cassie attended the sittings regularly over the next few weeks. Everyone agreed that she seemed well, vibrant with good health and energy. After awhile people stopped asking Cassie how she was doing, probably forgetting that she had been faced with a life-threatening illness. Even Aviva stopped talking about sending healing energy to Cassie. In the fall, Cassie missed several of the sittings. In late October, Tess told the group one Sunday that she had been worried and had called Cassie who said that she was fine, just busy with other things.

Over coffee, David said to Bill, "Do you think you should call her? You know, as her oncologist?"

"I'm in a bind about that," Bill said. "Normally, I would. Just have my nurse call and remind her that it's been more than three months since the last exam. But Cassie's not your average gal with breast c-a. She refused chemo before, got herself totally free of disease, as far as we could tell. I'm worried that if I call her, it might shake her faith in her ability to self-heal."

"You are one wise cancer doc," David said, hugging Bill. "Your patients are very lucky to have you. Besides, Cassie's a smart girl, right? And I bet her angels are smart enough to tell her to call you, if it were necessary." They both laughed.

✻ ✻ ✻ ✻

"When the student is ready, the teacher will appear."

That phrase from the previous Sunday's reading popped into David's head as he sat meditating in his car in the parking lot of Greenstar Natural Foods. He sometimes did this after a busy day at work, trying to clear his head, a transition before heading home. He opened his eyes, stretched, grabbed the grocery list off the dash, and turned to get out of the car. Then he noticed the young blonde woman in the next car smiling at him through the open window.

"Oh, my God, Cassie, how great to see you," he said.

They both climbed out and hugged. Cassie was wearing a long fall coat, but even through it, David could feel that she had lost weight.

"I was just leaving the market when I saw you in your car," Cassie said. "You looked so peaceful. There was no way I was going to interrupt you. So I waited to give you a hug."

"I hope it was worth the wait," David said, hugging her again.

"Totally," she said, laughing.

"We miss you," David said.

"And I miss you guys," she said. "It's just that I've been so …"

"I know, Tess told us. Busy, busy. Of course." David paused. They had stepped apart but were still holding each other's hands. David looked down. "Look, Cassie. What I want to say is, well, if you ever want to talk about stuff. You know, things that might be hard to talk about. As friends, I mean, not in the office. I'm pretty good at listening after all these years, and at not giving advice."

David looked up, into Cassie's eyes. They were brimming with tears, but she was still smiling. "I would like that, David. I think I would like that very much. Thank you. I'll call you."

A week later, after Cassie had missed another meeting of the group, David sat at his desk, his eye on the telephone. He picked up the receiver, dialed the first few digits of Cassie's number, then hung up. It's none of your fucking business, he told himself. You made the offer, she said she'd call, she didn't. End of story.

He reviewed his notes for the next patient.

He thought of writing her. *Cassie, sometimes the things we don't talk about can kill us.* Yeah, right, buddy. Who do you think you are, one of the angels? He paced the office awhile, trying to let go. He sat down again, pounded his fist on the desk. "I want to do the right thing," he said aloud to the room, his voice husky. He wondered who could tell him what was right to do. *No one I know*, he thought.

When the student is ready, the teacher will appear.

That night, just before midnight, the phone rang at his beside.

"Yes," David said softly, trying not to wake up.

"David, it's Cassie. I'm sorry to call so late. I was hoping you'd still be awake. Go back to sleep. I'll call you in the morning."

David could tell she'd been crying. He sat up, instantly alert.

"No, no, Cassie. It's fine. I'm glad you called. I'm really glad you called."

"I couldn't sleep. I haven't slept since …" She stifled a sob. "When do you think you might have time to talk? You know, as friends, like you said?"

"Do you know Al's All Night Diner? On the Boulevard? I'll see you there in a half hour."

David waited outside in a light drizzle, watching the neon *All* flicker and buzz. Finally it faded and died. "Al's Night Diner," the sign said.

Cassie pulled into the deserted parking lot, killed the ignition, but did not get out of the car. David walked over, stood next to the driver's door, his palm extended toward the entrance to Al's. Cassie rolled down the window and looked at him, shaking her head.

"I can't do this, David," she said.

David said nothing.

Slowly Cassie got out of the car. She was wearing a dark rain slicker, the hood pulled up and drawn close about her face. She let David guide her into the diner, to a corner booth near the restrooms.

They ordered coffee and sat silently until the waitress returned. Cassie kept the dark hood pulled up for awhile. She looked down at the table or at her hands in her lap. David was reminded of the sullen teenagers who sat in his office in their oversized sweatshirts, the hoods pulled up, their eyes cast down. Suddenly, as if she had come to some decision, she sat up straight in the booth, pulled off the hood and beamed her famous smile at him.

"Well, how are *you?*" she said brightly, fluffing her blonde curls with the fingers of both hands. Her green eyes sparkled at him.

They made small talk for awhile, smiling and nodding, until David pushed his cup aside and sat silently, his hands folded on the table. Cassie stopped talking and looked at him. Her smile faded briefly, then returned, like sunshine through high clouds, but she said nothing.

"Just tell me, Cassie," David said.

Cassie took in a ragged breath. The corners of her mouth turned down, her chin trembled.

"I wanted to be an actress," she said slowly. "I don't know if I could have made it, but I really wanted to try."

"What kept you from it?"

Cassie brought a clenched fist to her mouth and turned her head sideways. She seemed to be staring at the EXIT sign. Her shoulders heaved, but she made no sound. David cleared his throat and waited.

"He got me pregnant," she said, still staring at the sign. Suddenly she turned and faced David, her face dark. She spoke rapidly, in a fierce whisper. "He didn't use a condom, even though he said he did. He was afraid of losing me. I don't love him. I've never loved him. He must have known that. Even after the baby, I wanted to try, to go back and finish school, but he talked me out of it. 'We need you at home,' he always said. And when that didn't work, when I told him I was going back anyway, he lost his job. And then lost another one. Finally I started the children's center in our home. He worked for me. Then we built on, constructed a small theater. Cassie's Sunshine Center. Ha."

Cassie was not smiling. She looked much older, David thought, her eyes dark with rage and her mouth a thin, bitter line. He sat silently for awhile, hoping Cassie would continue, wondering what lay beneath the rage. Finally he spoke.

"Cassie, have you talked about this with Devon?"

"No. He couldn't handle it. It would kill him."

But this is killing you, he thought. *You must know that.* "Have you talked with a therapist?"

"What good would that do?" Cassie said. "It wouldn't change anything. Besides, they cost money."

"My God, Cassie. You have cancer. This is a matter of life and death. You have to do something about ..."

"You're yelling at me, David."

David paused, covered his mouth with the back of his hand, looked down at the table. "I'm sorry," he said, speaking softly. "I am angry. But Cassie, look, I have to ask you this: Do you want to live?"

Cassie's eyes softened. Her face seemed to relax.

She looks almost peaceful, David thought, *and very beautiful.*

"I don't think so," she said.

"I don't know what to say," he said.

"I know," she said. "That's okay." She stood up, preparing to leave. "Thank you, David. You're an angel."

*   *   *   *

When David entered the church for the memorial service, he saw the group sitting together near the back of the sanctuary. David hadn't attended a Sunday sitting for the few weeks before Cassie died. Her condition had deteriorated rapidly after their midnight chat. David of course had kept their meeting confidential. Tess and Bill had visited Cassie at home and reported back to the group that while she was bedridden and in obvious respiratory distress, she remained in good spirits, smiling, even laughing at times. They said that Devon was by her side constantly, holding her hand. He had told them that there was a daily stream of visitors—mothers and children mostly—from the center. They told Cassie, he said, that she had to hang in there and get well because what would they do without her.

On that Sunday, the last sitting that David had attended, Aviva proposed that they do a silent, healing meditation "for our brave Cassie."

"It doesn't sound like she could possibly recover at this point," said David. "I think Bill would agree that Cassie is terminally ill."

Bill nodded his agreement. Aviva smiled and spoke again. "Cassie may be getting ready to depart her physical body, David, which is all the more reason why she needs to heal. Healing is not the same as a cure. I suggest we direct our healing images, prayers, and energy toward her astral body. Her soul, if you will."

Bill rang the bell, and the group settled into the meditation. David tried, but could not get past his nausea. He sat quietly for as long as he could, then slipped away, out into the cold Sunday morning sunshine and took a few deep breaths. He hadn't returned to the group since that day.

David saw Alex waving to him from the back of the sanctuary, motioning him over. They all seemed glad to see him, welcoming him into the fold with hushed greetings and subdued smiles. An organ prelude signaled the start of the service.

They sat through hymns and readings that had been organized by the parish priest. Then a series of relatives, old friends, and associates spoke, some with voices clear and vibrant, declaring that Cassie had gone with her angels to a better life; others, in voices choked with emotion, saying how much they would miss Cassie. They all mentioned her famous smile, radiant and ever present. And they all talked about Cassie's remarkable devotion to the Sunshine Center and about the deep and abiding love between Cassie and Devon, which had sustained them both.

David sat with his head bowed, tears streaming down his face and falling onto the missal. He knew the others would think he was grieving for Cassie.

A Chink in the
Foundation

After the last two passengers squeezed past him, an apologetic old lady and a red-faced, sweating, fat man, Sherman lifted his suitcase onto the overhead rack. He felt the smear of dog shit on his hand even before he smelled it, and looking up, saw a dollop stuck to the side of one of the rollers. Holding his hand before him like a supplicant, he made his way to the bathroom, stepped gingerly around the puddle of urine on the floor and washed his hands in the tiny sink.

He attempted to clean the shit from the roller with several wet paper towels, but it was useless—the suitcase was history. His clothes would need to be switched to another container at the Amtrak station. As the train lurched and swayed northward, Sherman spent the next twenty minutes figuring out the logistics of the transfer. Satisfied with his plan, he reclined the seat, sighed, and rested his head against the cushion. He made a mental note to wash his hair as soon as he got to Priscilla's house.

He must have dozed, because his mouth was cottony, and a fragment of a recurrent dream clung to his eyelids. He was running barefoot from room to room, trying to find a clean place to relieve himself. As the pressure in his bowels mounted, the filth in the bathrooms multiplied. Finally he could stand it no longer. He waded in, despite the smeared feces and puddles of urine on the floor, and sat on the befouled toilet seat over a bowl overflowing with shit. As always, he awoke before letting go, before dropping his own shit on the world.

Priscilla's bathrooms, like the rest of the house and like Priscilla herself, were always sparkling clean and fresh smelling. Sherman recalled gentle, unperspired lovemaking atop fresh sheets, and showering again before sleep. He recalled how, in the morning they had brushed their teeth and drunk juice before conversing. Sherman smiled and felt a stirring in his penis. Eventually, Priscilla had left him and taken up with Mavis.

It was Mavis who had called him, telling him that if he wished to see Priscilla alive, he should come in the next couple of days. Christine encouraged him to go, assuring him that she and the kids could survive a weekend without him. She did not promise him that she would keep the refrigerator free of jellied fingerprints or the foyer floor mudless. Those were *his* jobs and anyway were trivial if you thought about an old friend dying of cancer, she said. Sherman knew she was right but couldn't let go of a tightness in his belly whenever he imagined the prints and the mud, which was often.

He tried thinking of Priscilla. He pictured her in the white, airy bedroom, lying in the four-poster they had shared so many years ago. She was covered with a floral duvet, her black hair splayed out against the plump off-white pillow. Her face was pale, but serene. She would smile a little when he walked in and extend a frail hand to him. It wasn't that he hadn't heard Mavis when she told him about the hair loss, the gray, bruised complexion, the tracheotomy requiring frequent suctioning, the feeding tube and the indwelling catheter. He had to see it his way, or he simply could not go.

The train braked suddenly, sending several bags flying from the overhead racks. Sherman braced himself with his hands against the seat in front of him. The woman across the aisle swore as her microwave pizza landed in her lap. The train came to a full stop, and the air brakes released with a loud hissing sound. Then complete silence in the car as if everyone was holding his breath, waiting to see what would happen next, quiet in anticipation of an explanatory announcement over the loudspeakers. None came. Sherman looked out the window at the darkened landscape. He could see only trees and a suggestion of water beyond them.

After a time, the passengers began talking among themselves, speculating on the cause of their delay, and a murmured consensus evolved. The train must have hit or nearly hit something on the tracks, and now the authorities were in the process of clearing it away. An announcement would be forthcoming.

Another fifteen minutes passed. Sherman could hear others on their cell phones, explaining and complaining to loved ones. The big man in front of Sherman got out of his seat and looked up and down the aisle. "Fuck this," he said under his breath and strode toward the front of the car. Sherman watched him punch the Push to Open pad on the door, which stayed closed. The man punched harder and kicked the door with his boot, but still nothing happened. Another man came up behind him and pointed out a lever above the door. He held the lever down while the first man attempted to wedge his fingers between the door and the frame. Nothing.

A southbound freight rushed past them in a whoosh of air and clatter, rocking the car. A baby in the rear began crying, then screaming, its mother helplessly shushing. The air around him grew stuffy, and Sherman began to smell other people—breath, farts, body odor, sicky-sweet perfume over unwashed skin. He opened a fresh container of Tic Tacs and held it to his nose, a temporary fix at best, he knew. He planned to stand between the coaches when the train got underway again, breathing the fresh air. And he would need to shower as soon as he reached Priscilla's. He rehearsed what he would say to Mavis.

The door at the front of the car slid open quietly, and a moment later, two bearded men wearing dirty work clothes, safety goggles, and muddy boots walked into the car. A few people behind Sherman cheered; someone shouted, "It's about time!" Another murmured, "Thank you, Lord."

The two workmen stood side by side, blocking the aisle. One of them unzipped his jacket and pulled a large pistol from the waistband of his jeans.

"Hey. Listen up, people. I'm only gonna say this once. Everbody stand, put your hands in the air, and turn toward the back of the train. Now!"

The passengers did as they were told. A woman sobbed softly.

The shorter bearded man, the one without the gun, proceeded down the aisle with a duffel bag, collecting money, cell phones, and valuables from each passenger. He appeared to be very polite. He approached Sherman, patted him down and took his wallet and cell phone.

"You have passport?"

"Yes," said Sherman, "in my jacket." He leaned over to retrieve his jacket from the seat next to him. He felt relieved. It was only a train robbery, like in the old days.

"Not now," said the man. "Keep hands in air." He looked down at Sherman's feet. "What is shoe size, please?"

"Eleven medium. That's about a forty-three in your country."

"Good," said the man and moved on to the next passenger.

Sherman watched to see if he asked anyone else for a passport or shoe size. He did not. The man completed his rounds, then came back up the aisle and stopped at Sherman's seat. He made an "after you" motion with his hand. Sherman frowned and shrugged.

"You. Into hallway please. Take jacket. Keep hands in air." He prodded Sherman along to the front of the car and made him lie face down in the aisle in front of the man holding the rifle. He then went back to retrieve the big man who had tried earlier to open the door, and made him lie next to Sherman on the floor. The man's heavy body pressed against Sherman, and his hot breath was in Sherman's face. Sherman needed to pee—badly. After what seemed like a very long time, he heard a whistle and a shout from outside the train. The man with the weapon ordered them to their feet and motioned them out the door and onto the platform between the coaches. The outer door was open but the steps had not been lowered.

Sherman gulped the fresh air and for a moment was grateful for having been one of those chosen. The man with the gun gave him a push.

"Off the train," he ordered.

Sherman grabbed the handrail and jumped down as gingerly as possible. The big man was right behind him, flying off as if he'd been shoved, then landing on his hands and knees in the gravel. He stood and examined his hands, cursing under his breath, then licked some gravel and blood off one of his palms.

"Take off your pants and shoes. Socks too. Then face them woods." The man with the gun sat on the edge of the platform pointing his weapon at them.

Sherman did as he was told, then stood looking into the darkness. He could make out a swampy area just beyond the railroad bed, then a narrow body of water, then the outline of some trees against the night sky. It occurred to him that they would be ordered into the swampy water and then shot, and he began to tremble. His bladder let go and he felt warm piss filling his boxer shorts and running down his leg into the gravel. Absurdly, he felt ashamed.

He heard the whistle and shout again, off to his left, then a flashlight beam appeared from near the front of the train and began to move toward him. As they got closer, the glow from the flashlight illuminated a small knot of shoeless, trouserless men, and behind them, more bearded men with guns. The man with the accent gathered all the pants, shoes, and socks, and placed them in the duffel bag along with the valuables. He also took Sherman's passport from his jacket pocket.

"Single file into the swamp. Keep your mouths shut. Anybody talks or bolts gits a bullet in the head, okay. Move out."

The half-naked men looked at each other. The big man shrugged his shoulders, then turned and marched into the swamp. Sherman was close on his heels. Mud oozed between his toes, and cattails whipped his bare legs. He stumbled on hummocks of clotted weeds. The air was close and smelled fishy. All was silent save for the sucking of feet through the muck and the harsh breath of men. A bullfrog croaked off to his right, loud enough to make him jump sideways.

When they reached the edge of the open water, the big man stopped, raised both of his hands, and looked around for the bearded man with the pistol. The gunman approached cautiously, keeping a distance between them.

"I can't swim," the big man whispered.

"Oh fuck that," the gunman said. "It ain't hardly up to your dick. Move out!"

The water was as warm as the air, maybe warmer, Sherman thought, and covered with patches of slimy, green algae that clung to his thighs. Still, he was grateful that his skin was being cleansed of the urine. He waded on through the big man's wake, perhaps fifty yards, until the water became shallow, and he felt submerged branches and the roots of trees beneath his feet.

When they reached dry ground, they were at the edge of the woods that Sherman had seen from the train. The group of men paused, looking around while the gunmen came up behind them.

"Keep movin'. Straight on. And don't git no ideas about runnin' off in them woods. We got boots and you ain't. We'll track you down."

The men moved slowly through the stand of old hardwoods, mostly beech and maple. The ground was rocky and uneven. Sherman winced and dipped as sharp edges dug into the soles of his feet. Low-slung branches clawed at his face and neck. They soon came to a clearing, and the men stopped again. Sherman could make out the roofline of a house against the darkened sky.

The man with the accent came up and led them toward the house, an old fieldstone building with thick walls and narrow windows low to the floor. At the back of the house was a heavy wooden cellar door, which the man lifted with considerable effort. He stood holding the lid open while the man with the flashlight motioned them in. As the last of the four captives descended the steps, the man handed him the flashlight.

"Not much juice left in it," he said, "but it beats nothing."

The man with the accent shouted down to them. "Please to take off rest of clothing and give up to me."

The men undressed and tossed their shirts, jackets, and sweaters out through the cellar door. Moments later, a pile of heavy clothes and boots landed at their feet. Then the lid slammed shut behind them, and they heard an iron bar slide into place followed by the click of a padlock.

"What the fuck?" said the big man.

"They gave us their clothes," said another voice in the dark.

"Now I get it," said Sherman. "Four of them and four of us. Each one of us was picked for our size. They're going to take off in our clothes. The one guy has my passport. And they've all got our wallets and cell phones. Talk about identity theft."

"Okay, genius," said a voice Sherman hadn't heard before. "Now can you get us the hell out of here?"

No one spoke. The air in the cellar was damp and clammy against their skin. With the aid of the flashlight placed on the dirt floor, they dressed quickly in the soiled work clothes and boots. Sherman swallowed a lump of disgust as he stepped into the filthy jeans and pulled on the sweaty socks of another man.

One of the men shone the flashlight around the cellar. The ceiling was low. The heavy hand-hewn floor joists not more than three inches above the big man's head. The room was bare except for an empty burlap sack cut open and spread out in one corner. On this makeshift tablecloth, their captors had left two loaves of white bread, a jar of peanut butter, and a table knife. Next to the food were two twelve-packs of bottled water.

"My guess," said one of the men, "is that they don't want us to die. They just want us stuck in here long enough so's they can get themselves out of the country or whatever before we can get to the police."

"You got that right," said the big man. "Now if only they'd gone ahead and left instructions as to how to get the fuck out of here. That food ain't going to last but a couple of days."

"That's right," said Sherman. "Here's my suggestion. Let's hold off on the food tonight. In the morning, probably some light will show through a chink in the foundation, indicating where the fieldstone may have shifted. Then, if we start taking turns digging with our hands and that knife over there, we should be able to make a big enough rent in the wall to crawl through to the outside."

"Good thinking, pal," said a man who hadn't spoken before. "What's your name?"

"Sherman."

"Mine's Robbie."

"Sal," said another.

"I'm Cletus," said the big man. "And I don't intend to spend the night here. Shine that light over on the trapdoor they shut on us."

Robbie shone the light on the overhead door and then on the six steps that led to the outside. The beam was already beginning to weaken and flicker. The big man stood on the bottom step, raised his arms and pushed against the slatted boards. The door creaked but didn't give an inch.

"Shit," he said. "Keep that light on the steps. I got an idea."

The big man crouched low and climbed the steps until he had wedged himself in between the steps and the lower end of the door where it met the ground. He put his back against the door, his hands on his knees, and strained upward.

"Give, you motherfucker, give," he shouted.

They heard a small cracking sound, and the big man fell facedown on the dirt floor, screaming.

"My back! My goddam back is broke. I can't move my legs!"

"Oh my God," said Robbie.

"He shouldn't have tried that," said Sal. "Let's try to get him turned over."

"No, no, no. Don't touch him," said Sherman. "You could make it lots worse." He went over and knelt next to Cletus, who was moaning and clawing the dirt. "Can you move your toes?"

"Yeah, a little. Is that good? I can't move my legs."

"Yes. It's a good sign you can move your toes. Try to relax and breathe. Get him a bottle of water, someone."

As he held the bottle to the big man's lips, Sherman suddenly smelled fresh shit, strong and foul. He gagged and covered his mouth and nose with his sleeve.

"I shit myself," said Cletus. "I'm sorry."

"Couldn't be helped," said Sherman, willing his voice to sound casual.

The flashlight beam flickered in Robbie's hand, then faded to a barely perceptible glow. "Oh, shit," said Robbie.

"Turn it off. Turn it the hell off," said Sal. "Give it a rest. It might come back."

Sherman took off his shirt, rolled it up, and placed it under Cletus' head.

"Thanks," said Cletus, "that helps. Guess we can't do nothing till morning."

"Hey, guys," said Sherman, "let's try to get some sleep. And listen, if you need to pee or shit, please go in the corner away from the food."

Sal laughed. "Yeah. Even dogs don't shit where they eat."

Sherman lay down in the dirt next to Cletus. He pulled off one of his work boots, used it for a pillow, and lay there staring into the darkness, alert, vigilant. He recalled an old war movie he had seen as kid. The troops were dug in for the night, waiting until dawn to move out. They couldn't even smoke because the light from the match might reveal their position. I could do that, he remembered thinking, back then.

He awoke to a feeling of pressure in his bladder and a sensation of heat on his left palm. He opened his eyes slowly and looked down at his hand. A slanted shaft of rosy gold had settled there. He noted how dirty his hand looked in the early morning light, but smiled a little, pleased to have slept. He glanced over at Cletus, who hadn't moved an inch and was asleep, breathing easily. Sherman could make out Sal in the far corner, squatting with his pants down around his ankles, and looked away quickly. The man deserved privacy. Robbie was still asleep, the meager flashlight clutched to his chest. In the near corner, one of the loaves of bread had been ripped open in the middle, several pieces strewn on the dirt floor, gnawed.

He heard Sal zip up his pants and move toward the center of the room. He sat up and yawned. "My turn in the outhouse," he said. "Well, inhouse, really."

"You sound pretty chipper, considering the shit we're in here," said Sal.

Sherman yawned again. "Hey, we got light, we got food and water, whatever the rats left us, and we got three men who are going to dig themselves out of this shit-hole right after breakfast. C'mon, Robbie, wake up and smell the feces."

Sherman limped over to the evacuation area, one foot in the thick-soled work boot, the other in a damp sock. As he took a step closer to where Sal had shit in the dark corner, his stockinged foot squished into something semisolid and slightly warm. *You should have put the boot on, asshole,* he told himself. He unzipped and pissed into the darkness. He stripped off the sock, tossed it in the corner, hobbled back, and put on the other boot.

Squatting down next to the burlap, he took a bottle of water, drank half of it, and rinsed his hands with the rest, drying them on his dirty undershirt. He made three peanut butter sandwiches and passed them around, ate his, then made another and took it over to Cletus.

"How are you doing, buddy," he said.

"There ain't no pain," said Cletus, "but I still can't move my legs."

"No, I see that," said Sherman. "We'll get you to a hospital as soon as we dig our way out of here."

"Sorry I can't help," said Cletus.

Sherman patted the big man's shoulder and handed him the sandwich and a water bottle. Then he got up and followed the shaft of sunlight over to the crevice that welcomed it. The opening, which was adjacent to where one of the massive floor joists was grooved into the sill timber, easily admitted three of his fingers. He tugged at a corner of one of the abutting fieldstones but couldn't budge it.

"Rock solid," he said aloud. He picked up the peanut-butter knife and a fist-size stone from the dirt floor and using the stone for a hammer and the knife as a chisel, began chipping away. Minute shards of stone flew at him and stuck to his face and neck, which were already sweaty from the sun and the effort of working with his hands above eye level. He peeled off his undershirt and fashioned a turban from it to help keep the sweat out of his eyes. After a time he stopped and looked at his left wrist where the Rolex had been before the man with the accent collected it. The watch had been a gift from Priscilla. Christine never said she resented it, but it occurred to him now that she might be glad to see it gone. So was he, in a way. He thought he'd probably replace it with a Timex, so he wouldn't have to worry about it.

"Hey, Sherman," said Robbie, handing him a bottle of water, "I'm ready to take a turn now."

"Thanks," said Sherman, guzzling the water and letting some of it run down his chin and neck.

"You look like a fucking A-rab," said Sal.

Sherman grinned and brandished the knife before handing it and the stone to Robbie. "Watch out for your eyes," he said.

He went over and sat down next to Cletus. Cletus motioned him closer and whispered. "If that fella' don't like Arabs, I wonder what he thinks of me." Cletus giggled like a schoolgirl.

"He's probably relieved you're down in the dirt," said Sherman.

"Yeah, but he better watch out. I ain't under it yet."

Both of them laughed aloud. "Hoo-eee," said Cletus.

Sal took his turn, and by the time the sun was more or less overhead, they were able to jiggle the stone a little. They chipped at it for another hour or two until they thought they might be able to pull it loose. Sherman and Robbie wrapped socks around their hands and grabbed corners of the stone, rocking it until it finally began to budge. After another round of chipping and rocking, it gave suddenly, falling at their feet and sending them flying backward onto the floor. Dusk poured in through the opening.

"Hoo-eee," shouted Cletus. "You guys okay?"

"I am," said Sherman. "Down but not out."

"Me too," said Robbie, "but I think I'm just gonna lie here awhile."

"Hey Sal," said Cletus. "How about pulling a few more stones loose? Should be easy now that first one's out."

"I'll do your share," said Sal.

"Um, yeah, that's good, Sal," said Sherman. "You know. Teamwork."

A few minutes later, when the opening was large enough for a man to crawl through, Sal stepped back from the wall.

"That'll do her," he said.

"Oh, man, we are so out of here," said Robbie.

"Free at last," said Cletus. "Except for me." He laughed without bitterness.

Sherman looked at the hole and felt an unaccountable sadness. He shook it off, jumped to his feet, and piled a few stones together so he could look through the opening. The tops of the trees glowed orange in the setting sun. The yard around the old house was overgrown with weeds, and a rusty tricycle lay tipped in the grass. He could make out a short driveway that led to a dirt road. He climbed back down and turned to the other men.

"I figure two of us should go for help. The other stays behind to look after Cletus until the EMTs get here. I can do that."

"That don't make sense, Sherman," said Robbie. "See, whoever goes is gonna need help to get up and through the opening. You and Sal are both pretty slim fellas. I should boost you up and then stay behind. Cletus and me will finish off the peanut butter."

"Okay with you, Cletus?" asked Sherman.

"I be okay alone far as that goes," said Cletus. "I trusts you to send help."

"That's all right," said Robbie. "I couldn't get out anyway without making that hole bigger, and it's getting dark and stuff, you know."

Sherman nodded. He put the filthy undershirt back on and took a swig of water. Robbie knelt down by the wall so Sherman could climb on his shoulders, and in a minute, Sherman was outside. He turned and gave a hand to Sal who was elbowing his way through the hole. Then he stuck his head back in.

"Hang in there, you two. Help is on the way."

He stood up and turned to Sal. "Which way you think we should go on that road?"

"Back in the direction the train came from," said Sal. "We passed a few small towns before we stopped. We don't know what's ahead."

"You can say that again," said Sherman. "Okay, let's move out. We need to find a telephone."

They started walking south on the road in the gathering darkness. There were no other houses, and no cars came by. After about half a mile, the road ended abruptly in a T at a two-lane stretch of macadam.

"Now we're talking," said Sal.

They walked east, away from the setting sun, and after a while, they heard the hum of tires behind them. They turned and stuck out their thumbs as the slow-moving vehicle drew near. It was a late model Ford pickup with a cap. It was too dark to tell for sure, but it looked like only a driver in the cab. The truck passed them, then pulled off on the shoulder, waiting.

Sherman ran ahead and stood near the passenger door. The window was rolled down a little, enough for Sherman to see the old man, both hands on the steering wheel and looking at Sherman out of the corner of his eye. He had not released the door locks, but kept shifting his gaze to the rearview mirror until Sal came up alongside the car. Then he sat staring at them, waiting.

"We're trying to get to a telephone," said Sherman.

He gave the old man an abbreviated version of their misfortunes and told him about Cletus back in the cellar. The old man said he didn't own a cell phone and couldn't think where there was a pay phone. He offered to take them to the state police barracks which he said was on Route 9, about fifteen minutes away, and they could tell their story to the troopers. "Get in the back," he said.

When they walked into the fluorescent-lit office, the sergeant took his feet off the desk in a hurry and put his hand on his weapon. They started to tell their story again, but the cop stopped them and asked if they were from the hijacked Amtrak train. He opened a folder and studied a FAX sheet, then told them their names and occupations and the names of their wives and kids.

"We're famous, huh?" said Sal.

"You smell like shit," said the trooper.

The trooper radioed for a police car and an ambulance to go to the farmhouse.

Sherman told him they'd need to take bolt cutters along for the cellar door padlock in order to get Cletus out of there.

"Now I need to ask you a few questions about the perps," said the sergeant. "They're probably out of the state by now, but you never know."

He pulled out a form from the top drawer and motioned Sal and Sherman into a pair of wooden chairs near the desk. When they sat down, he looked up and wrinkled his nose.

"You guys willing to take a shower before we proceed?" He jerked his thumb in the direction of a door behind the office. "We got some clean clothes and stuff back there."

"Oh, yeah," said Sal. "How about food? You got any of that?"

In the bathroom, as Sherman was about to step into the stall shower, he looked down at the sweat-soaked, shit-smelling pile of clothes he had just peeled off. He figured the troopers would just toss them in the garbage, but he wanted to ask if he could take them home with him, like a hunter takes home a boar's head. He remembered his grandfather showing him the swastika patch he'd taken off a dead German. But knew he wouldn't ask. No one would understand.

They were put up at a motel at government expense and given vouchers for food.

The next morning, when Christine drove up to get him, she brought along a suit of clothes, with fresh underwear and socks, his Cole Haan loafers, and a blue, button-down shirt of Peruvian cotton. She told him she liked the three-day growth of beard he was sporting and said that he sounded really relaxed, like he'd been at a spa instead of in a dark cellar. He smiled and said yeah. When she told him Mavis had called and that Priscilla had died the previous day, he just nodded.

It was getting dark when they got to the house and a light rain was falling, so Sherman stepped carefully on the flagstone path to avoid getting his loafers dirty. In the foyer he noticed a child's muddy footprint on the tile and made a mental note to get a wet paper towel from the kitchen and wipe it up.

Two Thousand
Blessings

Zebedee Minor paused at the top of the stairs and set the soup pot down with a thud. The stainless steel lid slipped off the pot and rolled on its edge over to the door to 2A where it announced itself in celebratory fashion, befitting the season.

"And happy fuckin' New Year to you too," shouted Belle Starr through the closed door. She appeared, before Zeb regained enough breath to speak, wearing black stockings, black garter belt, and a pink brassiere, and grinned toothlessly at Zeb. "I smell a free meal—where'd you get that, you old fart?"

"They's lots more down on the stoop. Chris Duguid is watchin' out nobody swipes it." Zeb paused to cough and hack up a gob of phlegm. "He give me a ride home from the mission with enough food to feed Cox's Army. Git them kids of yours to carry it up to my place and you can all feed yer faces, even Smitty."

Zeb replaced the lid and began to struggle up the next flight of stairs, narrower and darker than the first. By the time he reached his door, which was bedecked with a hand-lettered sign reading The Penthouse at Lincoln Arms, Belle's boys had passed him twice on the stairs, carrying trays, cardboard boxes, and clear plastic bags filled with food. Most of the other inhabitants of the Arms had also passed him on the way up and were now assembling in the Penthouse, except for Dolores Pratt who was too fat to squeeze past him and so puffed her way impatiently behind him.

Smitty had some wine, two gallons, in fact, of not-too-bad stuff that no one questioned the origins of, and the mission had sent plenty of plastic cups along with forks and spoons and napkins and even a real state fair carving knife. Lacking a table, they chased the cat into the hall and spread the food out on the floor. Belle's boys reached for it, but Zeb smacked their hands, announcing that he would lead them all in a toast to the new millennium.

Smitty filled the cups, and Zeb killed the lights and stood, his back to the one tiny window. The blue neon from Capitol Cadillac across the street flashed around the room, lighting up the faces of his friends. Zeb held his cup high and blessed them.

"Two thousand blessings on you all!" he said, and sat down.

"Hey, this stuff has got *labels* on it, Ma," said Belle's older boy, "want me to tell you what everything is?"

"Never mind that," said Dolores, reaching with her fork toward the nearest tray. This time, Belle smacked the fat woman's hand away.

"I got all gussied up for this feast, and I want to know what I'm eating, so yeah, Tony, read all the labels, nice and clear and slow." Belle was wearing a Kelly green, organdy bridesmaid dress, and she had her teeth in. She smirked at Dolores and winked at Zeb and sat down with a degree of gracefulness.

Tony crawled serpentine among the containers, reading as he went. "Turkey Breast. Baked Ham. Mashed Potatoes. Glassed Sweet Potatoes. Mixed Greens. Dee Jon Honey Mustard Salad Dressing. Diner Rolls. I can't read the label on the soup pot, Ma. I think Zeb slopped on it on his way up the stairs."

"Vichyssoise" said Zeb, perfectly.

*   *   *   *

The cabbie from City Taxi hopped and hitched his way up to the admitting desk at the emergency entrance to Saint Joseph's. He spoke around the cigar clenched in his teeth. "Somebody, quick, get this guy out of my cab. He shit all over the backseat and now he's lying in it, passed out."

"Want me to take a look at that leg of yours, sir?" said the third-year med student on ER rotation. She had expected a lot of action on New Year's Day, and so far it had been slow. The ER resident was asleep on a gurney in the corner, and the admitting clerk was filing his nails and making kissy noises into the phone. The cabbie ignored the student and blew smoke in the clerk's face, which got his attention.

"Sir, I'm afraid you can't smoke in here?" It came out as a question. "And may I see your insurance card, please?"

The cabbie leaned in close with his cigar breath and said something to the clerk. Moments later, two orderlies wheeled in the ashen gray, shit-stinking man, identified by a scrawled note pinned to his shirt as Smitty Smith of the Lincoln Arms. The ER resident awoke enough to get a line going in Smitty's arm and to hook him up to the monitors and call for GI and infectious disease consults. Massive bloody diarrhea was nothing to fool with.

By the end of the day, the med student had had all the action she could handle and was in the house staff bathroom vomiting and trying in vain to get the sick shit smell out of her nose and off of her new sweater. All the residents of Lincoln Arms, except for Zeb, had been admitted to the Infectious Disease Unit, and all were expected to pull through except for Smitty, who never made it out of the ER. The GI consult had told the resident who told the student who told Belle that his liver was too far gone to handle such a massive infection. Zeb sat and cried at Belle's bedside.

"My fuckin' blessing was a curse," he wailed. "I did this to all of you. Some fuckin' New Year."

Belle patted his hand and tried to smile. She told him later that she was grateful her boys didn't die.

Zeb sat with each of his friends, apologizing for his curse on them and promising to make it up to them in some way when they got better, until he finally fell asleep at the foot of Dolores' bed where he had knelt to pray. The night-shift aide, herself a graduate of the Arms, let him be, and called him a welfare cab before she went off duty at seven in the morning.

✳   ✳   ✳   ✳

Zeb was awakened midafternoon by a polite but persistent knocking on the Penthouse door. He admitted a pretty young woman in a short white lab coat, and a hard, gray lady in a public health nurse uniform. The young woman introduced herself as Dr. Mary Dolan from the local office of the CDC and explained that she was trying to track down the source of the pathogenic strain of E coli that had killed his friend Mr. Smith and sickened the rest of the residents of the Arms. Zeb, not fully awake, but recognizing an accusation when he heard one, began a tearful defense.

"Honest, lady, I didn't mean to curse them. All I said was two thous—"

"Mr. Minor," interrupted the nurse, "do you have any of the food left from New Year's Eve, or where did you throw … Oh my God, Mary, look!" She pointed to the floor near the window where a fat orange cat was picking delicately at a ham bone. "It's all there, right down to the soup the kid couldn't pronounce. I'll get the sample kit from the van."

Zeb lay back down on the mattress, turned his back to the doctor and pulled his holey army blanket over his head. The young woman asked him gently if he knew why he was the only one at the Arms who did not get sick, which Zeb took as further confirmation of his guilt.

He curled up into himself and made a high-pitched keening sound. The doctor persisted.

"Mr. Minor, please. Was there any part of the meal that you did not eat?"

"Vichyssoise—I hate the stuff," Zeb said.

*   *   *   *

Dr. Dolan smoothed her skirt and her hair as she passed through the wrought iron gates and under the granite arch at the entrance to The Townshend House. Before she could ring the bell, a small, leathery Asian man in a black suit opened the door and bowed almost imperceptibly in her general direction.

"Dr. Dolan, please come in. Mrs. Knox is expecting you." He motioned for her to follow him, and led her through a cavernous and darkened living room, a formal dining room—its long table set for one—and onto a small sunporch overlooking a grove of silver birch. The rays of a midafternoon January sun diffused through the crystal martini decanter, creating a rainbow on Mrs. Knox's white silk "at-home."

"Welcome to Townshend House, my dear." Mrs. Knox rose and after a momentary list to the right, stepped forward and extended her hand to the doctor.

"Harry, pour the good doctor a martini." She swept her hand in a graceful arc toward the wall of windows. "It was in this room, this small, simple room, that the general was inspired to write his memoirs of the Civil War. Sometimes I swear I can feel his presence when I'm alone in here." Mrs. Knox shivered a little and held her hands to her bosom.

"No, thank you, anyway," Mary said to the proffered drink. "I will have some tea, if it's not too much trouble."

Harry hurried off.

"Mrs. Knox, thank you for agreeing to see me on such short notice. As I mentioned on the phone, this deadly outbreak of E coli, which killed one man and has several others still in the hospital. Well, the soup that you and Mr. Knox donated to the rescue mission appears to have been the source of the infection. The CDC requires that I follow up on—"

"The vichyssoise! How dreadful. I mean it was simply awful. We just couldn't eat it at all. You see, Harry had prepared it according to Arthur's family recipe. The Knox family is notorious for their vichyssoise. Anyway, we had eight couples for dinner that night, and, of course, they were all expecting the vichyssoise. Why, we had no soup course at all, can you imagine!" Heather Knox wrung her hands and looked to Dr. Dolan for a sympathetic nod. "When Arthur tasted the soup just before our guests arrived, he spat it out and absolutely bellowed at poor Mr. Okari to get rid of the awful stuff. Well, I had Harry hide it on the back porch, and the next day I called the mission. I mean, hungry men don't need *perfect* vichyssoise."

Dr. Dolan, her voice tight and small, asked if she might ask a few questions of Mr. Knox, if he wasn't too busy. Harry had reappeared with the tea, but the doctor left it unsampled on the glass end table.

"Why, Arthur is in the hospital. Didn't I tell you on the telephone?" Mrs. Knox, seeing the doctor's stricken expression, added hastily, "Oh, he's not sick, thank goodness. He's just having a chin tuck—his third, between you and me, dear." Mrs. Knox stroked her own wrinkle-free neck with her withered hand. "Perhaps you can catch him there. He's at St. Joe's, plastic surgery, Dr. Witherspoon's service."

*   *   *   *

Zeb squeezed Tony's hand and told him that he was going to be just fine and that the doctor was going to allow Belle to visit him today. Then he picked up the large plastic shopping bag which held his army coat, woolen cap, mittens, and pac boots, and went out to the nurses' station to thank his old friend Hernandez for taking such good care of Tony.

Hernandez and another aide were eavesdropping on a conversation between a tall, silver-haired physician with bushy eyebrows and Ellen Kuhn, the charge nurse. Zeb waited and listened. Ellen was speaking.

"So you're telling me that *the* Arthur O. Knox came in for a routine plastic job and had a massive stroke during the procedure? My God, I'd hate to be in Witherspoon's shoes!"

The doctor nodded vigorously and grinned.

When the doctor left, Zeb tugged at Nurse Kuhn's sleeve. "Is that the Arthur O. Knox up to the Townshend House?" he asked.

Ellen was used to seeing Zeb around the pediatric ward, visiting Tony and his brother, and she smiled at him, though keeping her distance. "Yes, it is. Why, is he a friend of yours, Zeb?" She winked at Hernandez and retreated to the medication closet.

Zeb grinned at Hernandez. "Frankie, that's the guy I told you about, remember? That Chink fella Harry Okari who works for him up to Townshend House once hired me to do some prep work in the kitchen for him, seeing as I was a cook in the service and all. He used to make this stupid vichyssoise all the fuckin' time, and I had to peel fifteen pounds of goddam potatoes. I told him in the army I allus had a E-1 to do that scut work, but he still made me do it. I didn't last very long there. Fuckin' vichyssoise."

Zeb leaned against the nurses' desk and shook his head as if he still couldn't believe it. "Ya know, Frankie, the old guy never even looked at me when he come in the kitchen to check on the soup. Like I was indivisible, it was. What an asshole."

"Yeah," said Hernandez. "Well, he's gettin' his comeuppance now, I figure."

Zeb sighed. "Still, I kinda feel sorry for the old guy. All that money didn't do him no good. What ward you think he's in, Frankie?"

Hernandez explained that those people had their own private rooms, but that now that the rich bastard had had a stroke, he was likely in the intensive care unit like anyone else. Zeb thanked him and, stowing his bag behind the nurses' desk, he took the elevator up to the ICU. He paused outside the entrance and looked around. No one seemed to be watching him. He donned a mask and gown from the shelf and strode through the swinging doors, indistinguishable now from the rest of the staff. He made his way down the narrow aisle separating the two rows of beds until he came to the name tag reading: Arthur O. Knox.

The old man was alone except for an impressive variety of vigilant mechanical devices that were constantly commenting on his status. Zeb moved close to the head of the bed where he could see Knox's face, which to Zeb looked the same as it did twenty years earlier, except for the tubes running into or out of his nose and mouth. The old man's eyes were open and stared hopefully at Zeb. Zeb laid a warm hand on Knox's arm and smiled at him behind the mask.

"Two thousand blessings on you, sir," he said.

Sustenance

I knew Abe Needleman's face, and this was not it. This was the face of a toothless, dying old man, parchment skin hanging from bony ridges, mouth agape in a demented grin, eyes looking halfway to heaven.

"Uncle Abe," I shouted, "can you hear me?"

His eyes shot open and slashed me, like years ago, with that blue warning light. I drew back, fast, as if I still had something to fear.

"You think I'm deaf?" He looked around the room. "What's this place?"

"It's a hospital, Uncle Abe. You're very sick," I said.

He waved the back of his hand at me, dismissing the whole notion and probably me along with it. Me and my cockamamie ideas.

His landlord had found him on the floor, barely conscious, one hand clutching a yellowed envelope stuffed with hundred dollar bills. In the emergency room, he had refused to sign permission for any tests or procedures, but he would accept an IV, he'd told them. "Don't try to slip in any drugs with that," he warned. He had listed me, his only living relative, as next of kin.

"You seem determined to die, Uncle Abe," I said.

"What a genius," he said. "It's good you're a psychiatrist."

I could be pretty damned determined myself, when I felt like it. I persisted. "So you just stopped eating, huh? That'll work."

I'm especially determined when my curiosity is aroused, and I thought of this as a diagnostic challenge. Also it couldn't hurt to peel back another layer of the onion, find out more about what kind of stock I come from. If I couldn't help Uncle Abe to live longer, maybe he could help me to die better. Besides, he loved talking about himself.

He was the greatest all-around athlete in the history of his high school. He played golf with Bob Hope at Pebble Beach, tennis with Don Budge at Forest Hills. He was the first guy in Stuyvesant County to own a Ford Thunderbird. Just ask him. And if he got started on the babes, you'd better plan for a long evening. I decided to play that card.

"The girls are going to miss you," I said. This was not a lie. It was not one of those cute things people say to old men in nursing homes, with a sly grin and a wink at the relatives.

They would miss him. I had visited him a couple of months before, driven down one summer day to take him out to lunch. First he had to stop at the bank. We had to go inside, he told me, and we had to wait for Candy, the only one he trusted, he said. He leaned in toward her across the counter and said something. Whatever it was, Candy actually blushed. "Abe," she said, "you're some guy."

At the Valley Diner, we sat in his usual booth. Before taking our order, Andrea sat down next to him, close, and held his hand. He kissed her cheek. "Your uncle," she said to me. "If I wasn't married ..."

Later, I dropped him at the club and hung around awhile. Frankly, I wasn't sure I believed that he was still teaching racquetball. But there it was, a class of six women around forty-something, hanging on his every word. When one would miss a shot, he'd go up to her, stand close behind her, one arm around her waist, the other guiding her hand in a corrective arc.

"Get it?" he'd say.

"Got it," she'd say, smiling at him. The smile broadened when he patted her tush.

I sighed and left. I could never get away with that.

"I know," he said now. "I hate letting them down." Abe turned over on his side, facing the wall.

"By the way," I said. "Why aren't you wearing your dentures?"

He turned over so fast, the IV pole started to fall. I jumped up and righted it, then reached down to check the tubing in his arm, but he snatched his hand away.

"What the hell is wrong with you?" he said. "I never had dentures."

"The last time I saw you, last summer, those weren't … I mean, they were all your own teeth? That's amazing."

"Nothing amazing about it," he said, turning again toward the wall.

"Well then, what happened? Two months ago you had a full set, now nothing?"

"They quit on me. Just fell out."

"All of them, all at once?"

"One by one. What does it matter." He sounded very tired.

"Ah-ha," I said, sounding like a shrink with an insight. I gave myself a mental kick in the butt. "So that's why you stopped eating."

"Nah, I could eat without 'em." Abe curled up in the bed, his back to me. He offered no further comment.

I sat quietly, watching the IV drip. I remembered Uncle Abe smiling at the girls. A smile of pure pleasure, delight shining in his eyes. When I'd done something right by him, the best I ever got was a grudging grimace.

I understood now, or at least I thought I did, and it filled me with sadness. The girls nourished and sustained him. They were his daily bread. But he knew better than to go near them without his teeth. They would fuss over him, taking pity. He'd rather be dead.

"Uncle Abe," I said, "who was the girl you met at Grossingers? The one you brought up to our house right after the war."

"Lucette," he said. "Lucette Millman." He turned on his back and gazed up at the ceiling fan. "Now that was a dame. I dated her for three years. What a looker. Nice girl, too. Your mother nagged me to marry her. Why the hell would I want to get married, I told her. Sit around and watch it all turn to shit. No thanks."

"Did you ever meet Mona?" He propped himself up in bed and looked at me. I shook my head.

"Too bad. A dancer from the Copa. Legs up to here. Wherever I took her, guys would stare, green with envy. A pretty good tennis player, too. Not bad at all for a girl. She was always tan, you know, for the Copa. She looked smashing in white."

"I did meet another one though," I said. "Let's see, I was in college in New York, and you took me and my date out to dinner. This girl was with you. I don't remember my date, but I sure remember yours. What was her name? She had a blonde pony tail and big hazel eyes you could fall into."

He sat straight up in bed, a bit of color returning to his face. "Yeah, yeah. We went to Tooley's Steak House on Tenth Avenue. Her name was Penny, Prentice Hall. Beautiful girl. Smart too, college material. I remember she said something, then you said 'bright as a penny.' I thought, boy has he got a lot to learn."

"Uncle Abe, tell me about the time you danced the rumba with Rita Hayworth. You know, at the Nevele."

"Yeah, sure, boychick. But listen, first I want you to run over to the Valley and get me a corned beef on rye. Sauerkraut and Russian. Not too thick. There's money in my pants, over there in the closet."

"It'll be my treat, Uncle Abe," I said.

Good Neighbors

Marty Rothman sat uncomfortably outside the entrance to Hearing Room B in the Taghkanic County Courthouse. Behind the frosted glass door, the case of the People versus Delbert Perkins was being presented to the grand jury, the prosecutor seeking charges of second-degree murder against Delbert for the death of Robert Singh Khalsa (nee Robert Rosenthal, DOB 2/27/59, expired 10/17/01).

The bench was hard, unyielding, a Victorian relic designed, it seemed, to foil any attempt on Marty's part to relax and clear his mind. He desperately wanted to present the facts lucidly, to dispassionately reveal the events of October 17 as he had witnessed them, indeed, had been a part of them, so that the grand jury would come to the same conclusion that Marty himself had. Instead, his unruly brain produced only repetitive images of a dreaded emotional outburst in the courtroom.

"Can't you see? No one is guilty. Delbert would never have pulled the trigger. I made him do it. I panicked and pushed him. It's my fault Bob Singh is dead. Delbert, why he saved my son's life!"

To soothe himself, Marty paced and thought about his son Carl. He hoped the hearing would be over in time for him to get back to the farm and take Carlie into town for trick-or-treating. The local paper, in a flag-draped editorial, had recommended suspension of

Halloween activities in deference to the events of 9/11, but Marty, a child psychologist, felt differently. While he, like everyone else, was outraged by the attack, Marty knew that children needed the reassurance of routine, especially at times like these.

Carl was seven, the same age Marty had been when he first met Delbert. Marty's mom had made a loaf of banana-nut bread for Eloise Perkins to thank her for rescuing Ticker, their black Lab, from a coon trap that had been set in a culvert. The Rothmans had been living on the farm only for a week, as yet unaware of the hazards of rural life. When Eloise had brought Ticker back, she'd said, without a trace of sarcasm, "Most folks out this way keep their dogs to home."

Marty had taken the bread over to Mrs. Perkins on his bike, and when he handed it to her, she asked if he could stay awhile and play with her son Delbert, who was also seven. She told Marty he'd find Delbert down behind the barn, watching his dad and his uncle fix the barn roof.

"You that new kid?" Delbert yelled down to Marty from the second-to-the-top rung of a rickety, wooden, forty-foot extension ladder. Marty nodded and looked down at the ground again quickly. "C'mon up," Delbert said. "Dad says I can't get on the roof, but we can watch from here." Marty's stomach churned, and he wasn't sure his breakfast would stay down.

"I got to get back and help my dad with some chores. I'll see you later," Marty had yelled, his voice squeaky and unconvincing.

*   *   *   *

The door to Hearing Room B opened, and an old man in coveralls came through it slowly, shaking his head. Marty recognized him as one of Delbert's uncles who lived alone in a doublewide on the Perkins' farm. They nodded to each other. It was hard to tell, but Marty thought he was Hank, the brother that used come over with Mr. Perkins to help Marty's dad during that first winter when it seemed like the Buick was stuck in the snow more often than not. They'd bring a tow chain and hook it to the drawbar on the International and pull the car out like it was a child's toy. His father, Dr. Rothman, tried, at least the first time, to pay the men, but Dave Perkins waved one hand in the air as he climbed back into the tractor cab. "That's what neighbors are for," he said. Marty and Delbert had helped by throwing ashes from the woodstove under the tires of the Buick. Delbert seemed never to worry about getting too close to the churning rear tires of the heavy station wagon.

Helping out a neighbor wasn't all a one-way street. Delbert's sisters had asthmatic attacks, especially on cold mornings when they had to help with the milking before school. Marty's dad, half-dressed, bare feet in overshoes, would rush over to administer adrenaline and reassurance. More often than not, the girls managed to make the school bus.

"They're a hardy lot," Dr. Rothman said to Marty and his mom over breakfast. "I wonder if they had any medical care at all before we moved out here."

*   *   *   *

Don't you see? Delbert's that kind of guy, never giving a thought to himself when a neighbor's in trouble. Just like his dad was. Someone like that wouldn't shoot anyone. He only meant to scare Bob Singh. Del was really upset about 9/11. All those flags on his truck, and that bumper sticker. He probably thought Bob was a Muslim, with that turban. He was trying to make a citizen's arrest. Hold him for the sheriff, you know, for questioning.

It was just ignorance, Marty thought. Like the time Delbert's dad made that remark to my dad. Dave Perkins had been telling Doc about the new brush hog he had just purchased from the John Deere dealer. "Fellow wanted six-fifty with my old one on a trade-in, but I jewed him down to five hundred even. The prices these days will kill you," said Dave.

"Everything costs money," Dr. Rothman had said, looking at the horizon.

That evening at dinner, Marty had asked his dad if he thought Mr. Perkins hated Jews. Marty's mom put down her fork and stared at her husband, waiting for his answer.

"I'm sure Dave Perkins has no malice toward us, and I doubt that he even knows what the expression means. Besides, I think he may have said 'chew him down.'"

"Appeasement," said his mom. "Is that the message you want to give to our son? What if you had been a black man when Dave made that *jungle bunnies* comment last fall, remember, when he had to take Eloise to the Albany Medical Center? He took his handgun along, for God's sake."

There was more to the argument, but Marty had tuned it out. But in his friendship with Delbert, he had learned to avoid certain topics. In high school, when they smoked a little weed together behind the barn, Marty had giggled and said, "Rockefeller's going to have us both in jail for life."

"He's a good man," said Delbert, without a hint of irony. "Goddam dope fiends ought to be behind bars." Marty had exhaled with a cough, but said nothing.

And just last year, Marty remembered, he and Delbert had been hunting together in the hardwood triangle where both their properties abutted the Billings farm. Delbert heaved a rock over the barbed-wire fence into the neighbor's cornfield.

"Timber thieves," he yelled into the air. Marty had heard the tale many times. Delbert always spoke of it as if it had happened yesterday, instead of two generations previously.

"Geez, Delbert, maybe they just didn't know back then where the property line was," Marty said.

Delbert had shot him a look that said, "You're either with us or against us."

*   *   *   *

A gray-haired gentleman in a dark suit and tasseled loafers, who had been waiting on the bench opposite Marty, answered his cell phone. "Dr. Childers," he said.

Marty recognized the name. It was the orthopedic surgeon who had treated Delbert's fracture that past summer. It had never healed properly.

Didn't you see him walk—that terrible limp? He's crippled for life because he tried to save my son's life. A guy like that. I mean Bob Singh should not have come out here wearing that turban, especially during hunting season when everyone out here carries guns, and especially after 9/11. Who knows what Delbert thought when he saw Bob running up my driveway? I mean, if I didn't know Bob …

That past summer, in early July, Carl had climbed into the hayloft of the old, abandoned horse barn that still stood near the edge of the dirt road that bisected the Rothman farm. The Rothmans were meaning to tear down the crumbling ruin but hadn't gotten around to it. Carl managed to get into the loft by climbing the creaky handmade ladder, but when he looked down through the gaping floorboards, he was afraid to come down. Marty and his wife, Sue, were up at the house. When they heard Carl crying and yelling, they rushed across the road and into the lower level of the barn. "Don't worry, Carlie," Marty had said, "everything's fine. Daddy's coming up to get you." He had yanked a piece of rope off a rusted pulley and started cautiously up the shaky ladder to the loft.

Before Marty had gotten halfway up, he heard the loud whine of an ATV outside the barn. Then the engine was cut, and he heard Delbert say, "I'll get him, Sue. You stay down there."

Marty had continued up the ladder, and just as his head cleared the trapdoor, he saw two-hundred-and-twenty-pound Delbert bounding into the loft from the east end of the barn. Marty figured he had somehow carried an extension ladder on the ATV, leaned it against the exposed side of the old barn, and scrambled up.

Marty yelled to him from the ladder. "Hey, Del, the floor joists are rotten. I can get him from this end."

But Delbert had just kept running across the loft as if he'd never heard Marty. When he got to within three feet of Carl, one of the joists gave way, and Delbert dropped like a sinker to the cobblestone floor of the lower level. Marty heard Sue scream and then Delbert yell.

"Darn, my leg's busted!"

Marty had continued up through the trapdoor, tied the rope under Carl's arms, and lowered him down to Sue.

The next day, Sue was talking to Bev, Delbert's wife, about the incident. Delbert was in the hospital with a compound fracture that had to be surgically reduced by Dr. Childers. Bev said she knew that Delbert would do it again. In a heartbeat, she had said. She said that helping out a neighbor was just what you did.

"If they were good neighbors," she said, smiling.

Marty had visited Delbert in the hospital. Delbert was dozing, his left leg in a cast that extended halfway up his torso. Marty rapped on the plaster. "Oh, man, look at this," he'd said.

Delbert opened his eyes and grinned at Marty. "Those are the breaks," he'd said. Marty had started to say something about being incredibly grateful and about how sorry he was that Delbert was injured so badly, but Delbert had begun fussing with the controls on his bed stand and looking out the window. Instead, they talked about how to get the old barn torn down before winter set in.

✳   ✳   ✳   ✳

Don't you see? If Delbert had known Bob Singh the way I did, this never would have happened. Delbert likes everyone unless ... well, unless they've done something wrong. I mean, Bob didn't do anything wrong, but Delbert saw that turban and put two and two together and came up with

*five. And if Bob hadn't kept running when Delbert told him to stop ...
even then, Delbert would have just fired into the air to scare him. I was
the one who panicked. I slammed into Delbert's bad leg and the gun went
off.*

Marty got up from the bench and walked down the wide
marble-floored hallway to the men's room. He stood at the urinal and
looked down at the black-and-white checkerboard tile lining the floor
and the wall up to the wainscoting. He'd seen that old-fashioned tile
before. He remembered the bathroom in the Rosenthal's city flat,
where he and Bobby used to pee together, seeing who could make it
last longer.

And he and Bobby had started Hebrew school together. Already
Bobby was the scholar, helping Marty, whispering prompts into his
ear when the rabbi called on him to read a difficult passage. They had
remained friends even after they were no longer neighbors, after the
Rothmans moved to the farm. Bobby used to come out and spend
weekends. One time they had even played together with Delbert.

They lost touch with each other when Bobby's parents got him
into Andover. Marty heard that Bobby had gone on to Princeton and
graduated with honors. And then Bobby had called him shortly after
Marty had completed his PhD. Bobby said he had spent two years in
India and was eager to talk about his experiences with his old friend.
So Marty had driven into the city and showed up at the Thai restau-
rant at the agreed-on time, but he couldn't find anyone who looked
like Bobby Rosenthal. Then this tall, smiley fellow with a black beard
and a turban came over and gave him a bear hug.

"Nu, Rosenthal, that's quite a yarmulke," Marty had said.

Bobby pressed his hands together and bowed slightly. "No longer
Rosenthal, my friend. I'm Robert Singh Khalsa now. I've become a
Sikh. Let's sit—I'll tell you about it."

Before they parted after a long lunch, Bob Singh said that he'd
love to see the farm sometime, and Marty had nodded, but somehow
had never found the right time to invite him out. Until this October.
All those turbaned fellows on TV being called evildoers. Marty knew

it wasn't that simple, but he couldn't quite sort it out. He was sure his old friend would have a fresh perspective on the whole thing.

When he called to invite Bobby to the farm, Marty suggested leaving the turban at home. Bobby had laughed and said, "It's part of my religion, my friend. It's who I am."

Marty washed his hands and splashed water on his face. *I should have told Delbert that Bobby was coming out,* he thought. *Delbert has never had any doubts about who the bad guys are.*

Marty arrived back at the waiting area to find a young court attendant in a blue uniform and silver badge looking for him. "Dr. Rothman?" she said. "The grand jury is ready to hear your testimony."

Levels
of Consciousness
1959

"Charlie, go up and see the rabbi," said his father, "I'll stay here with Marion."

Dr. Goldberg, as he was now called, winced and swore under his breath. He was hoping his dad had forgotten about the rabbi's surgery. He had not seen the rabbi in the five years since poor Marion's bat mitzvah, and he did not miss the old man. Charlie had not forgotten about the day the rabbi caught him behind the schul playing mumblety-peg with Joey Martino when he was supposed to be in Hebrew School; the rabbi had dragged him by the ear into the breath-befouled classroom, shades drawn against the glorious April sunshine, and forced him to read aloud from a passage he had never seen. He remembered that day well, the day he had suffered enough humiliation in front of that group of snickering scholars to assign to the rabbi the dubious distinction of being the first Jew on Charlie's shit list.

Charlie still feared the rabbi's wrath. But not as much as the wrath of his father, so he boarded the elevator reserved for house staff and got off at the nine west surgery unit. The charge nurse, Herlihy, greeted him with the special disdain she seemed to reserve for nonsurgical residents.

"And what would a baby-bouncer like yourself be wanting in men's surg, might I inquire?" she said.

"I'd like to see Rabbi Gutmacher—he's a friend of the family." Charlie's smiled, a grimace involving only his mouth.

"Still in recovery." Herlihy jerked her thumb toward the ceiling without looking up from her notes. She spoke again. "How's that sister of yours?"

"Still in a coma." Charlie turned toward the stairwell that led to the recovery room, wondering how she knew about Marion. Herlihy called after him.

"Goldberg, I hope she does okay. I specialed her one night when she was first admitted to neuro; beautiful lass. Give my best to your parents."

"Thanks, Miss Herlihy. Thanks a lot," Charlie said, hurrying away before she could see the tears.

He paused at the top of the stairs to reapply his doctor face before entering the recovery room. He adjusted his tie, closed the button on his crisp white lab coat, and draped the stethoscope conspicuously around his neck. This done, Charlie was satisfied that there would be no question in the rabbi's mind about who he was dealing with. "See, Rabbi, no more little Charlie the Hebrew *bucha*."

At the nurses' station, Charlie pulled the rabbi's post-op chart from the rack and perused it with clinical detachment. He learned that the prostatectomy had been uneventful, no sign of prostatic cancer, no excessive blood loss, no complications of anesthesia. According to the note written and signed by Harry Millner, MD, chief of urological services, the patient was discharged from the OR to the recovery room in good condition.

As Charlie approached the bedside and noticed that the rabbi was still asleep, it crossed his mind to slip away and tell his father that he had seen the rabbi and that he was doing well. Just then the rabbi looked up at him, his eyes sad, kind, peaceful.

"Hi, Rabbi, remember me … Charlie Goldberg." Charlie thought his voice sounded distressingly small and young.

The rabbi's face brightened, and he motioned Charlie closer, taking his hand. Of course he remembered. He began to talk about things that Charlie had forgotten, like his bar mitzvah speech that Charlie had written in iambic pentameter and which was irreverently devoid of thank-yous.

"I liked that," the rabbi said, "a breath of fresh air."

The rabbi looked away and sighed heavily. He spoke of Charlie's sister Marion: her high school graduation last month, the head-on collision that same evening, the coma now in its fourth week, the congregation praying for her recovery.

Charlie felt the tears rising up again and abruptly changed the subject. "Well, Rabbi," he said in a tone that he hoped was professional, "you seem to be doing very well. Dr. Millner is the very best and, of course to him, this is a very, very routine procedure. I'm sure you'll be back on the *bimeh* in a week or two."

The rabbi responded slowly, his eyes hazy. "Well, I don't know about me. I feel old and tired. But your sister, Marion, she's going to be okay."

Charlie thanked the rabbi for his good wishes and left the recovery room.

How silly, he thought, as he waited for the elevator. *He probably just meant to say "I hope she's going to be okay." I mean everyone knows that her prognosis is poor. There's almost no chance of her recovering anything like normal functioning. How could he even think she would be okay? But, at least he was nice.*

Moments later, Charlie stepped off the elevator on 3 South and headed for his sister's room, prepared to report to his father the clinical details of his visit to the rabbi. He certainly was not going to say anything about the rabbi's absurd prediction.

As he neared, Charlie noticed a lot of activity outside the door to Marion's room. Movement, more people, excited voices. He saw his father rushing toward him, shouting.

"Charlie, Charlie, come quickly! She's awake!"

Standing at Marion's bedside, Charlie grinned at his little sister and said, "Where the hell have you been all this time?" It was an old family joke. Marion smiled with the left side of her face and squeezed Charlie's hand.

His mother was crying, then laughing, then crying some more and hugging everyone in the room, which was now filled with nurses, aides, house staff and other patient's relatives. Charlie went over to the chief of neurosurgery, who was still in a scrub suit, and pumped his hand.

"Thank you, Dr. Marlowe," he said. "Thanks so much for everything you've done. I just knew she'd pull through."

"I am totally and completely amazed and delighted," said the surgeon in his charming drawl. "It is, of course, too early to be certain, but I suspect she'll regain full function. It's like a miracle! Surely someone has been praying for her."

Charlie nodded respectfully but said nothing. He promised Marion he'd return at lunchtime, then headed down the corridor toward the pediatric unit where he was due to present a case at morning rounds. The squawk box, which had been blaring incessantly all morning (Dr. Webley, call 8 South, Dr. Webley ... X-ray tech to the ER stat ... Dr. Patterson, call the switchboard ...), suddenly caught Charlie's attention.

"Code blue recovery room ... Code blue recovery."

Charlie began to tremble. He attempted to continue on his way to rounds but an impulse propelled him to the nearest set of stairs, and he ran up the six flights to recovery. Breathless, he yanked open the door and nearly collided with Nurse Herlihy, losing his balance. Herlihy reached out and steadied him.

"Dr. Goldberg," she said. "I'm afraid he's gone. A massive pulmonary embolus, poor man. I'm so sorry."

Charlie nodded and tried to speak, but no words came. He turned back into the stairwell and began to descend slowly, carefully, like a much older man. He stopped on the first landing and looked around to make sure he was alone, then covered his head with his handkerchief, clasped his hands together, and began to rock gently. *"Yisgodol v'yiskodosh sh'mei rabbah ... "*

Immersion

On the drive there through the rolling Berkshire hills, Ida kept glancing nervously toward the backseat. Charlie was curled up in a ball, his head on the canvas duffel bag, pretending to be asleep. Charlie had never been to camp before. He had never even stayed overnight at a friend's house. Charlie was pretty much of a mama's boy. Uncle Al, his mom's big brother, had told Ida that her boy was a sissie, and if she didn't want him to grow up to be light in the loafers, she and Morrie ought to do something about it.

"We tried, Al," Ida had said, "we really did. Morrie took him to Cub Scouts, but Charlie came home crying because he got a stomachache on a nature hike."

"Cub Scouts," said Al, sneering. "More sissie stuff. Look, Ida, my friend Nat Holman runs a basketball camp in Hillsdale. I'll pay for it. You just get him there."

When they reached Camp Scatico, Charlie and Ida both had to use the bathroom, badly. At the office, a guy with a whistle around his neck pointed Charlie toward the outhouse in back and told Ida she could use the lavatory in the infirmary. Ida whispered something to the man. He shrugged, turned up his palms, then directed both of them toward the infirmary.

"It's nice in here, Mom," said Charlie. "It smells like Dr. Buddy's office."

Ida patted him on the head and let him go first. She stood near the door, listening for diarrhea.

At noon, a loudspeaker announced that it was time for all parents to leave. Ida hugged Charlie, tears streaming down her face. Charlie stood stiffly, looking down at his shoes, then he watched until the green Buick was out of sight.

Charlie walked back to the Lions bunkhouse to which he had been assigned along with eleven other boys. He found his bunk with his camp trunk and duffel that Morrie had carefully stowed under the bed and began to unpack his clothes. The kid at the next bunk pointed at Charlie's slippers and laughed, inciting other kids to join in. Charlie put his head down and continued unpacking. Morrie had always told him to ignore rude boys.

A counselor whose name tag said Jerry came over to Charlie and laid a gentle hand on his shoulder.

"Need any help unpacking, buddy?" said Jerry.

Charlie liked being called buddy and wondered how the counselor knew that. He looked up gratefully at Jerry and almost smiled. He sighed. "I guess I can manage," he said. "But thanks."

After lunch, they chose up sides for the scrimmage. Charlie and a fat kid were the last to be chosen. Uncle Al had given Charlie a basketball for his birthday that past spring and had taken him out behind the house and drilled him for hours, passing, receiving, dribbling, layups, set shots. "You'll do fine," he told Charlie.

But Charlie wasn't doing fine. On the rare occasions when one of the other kids passed the ball to him, he dropped it. He tripped over his own feet while dribbling. He tried guarding his opponent closely, but the kid knocked him down.

Jerry came over and picked him up. "Hang in there, buddy," he said.

Charlie lay on his bunk after the scrimmage, staring up at the rafters. When they went to dinner, he held his stomach, moved his food around on the plate. After dinner, when they were supposed to be watching a movie of the Knicks versus the Celtics, Charlie told Jerry that he felt sick and wanted to go to the infirmary.

"Listen, buddy," said Jerry. "You've had kind of a rough first day—right? Here's what I want you to do. Forget the stupid movie. Go to bed and get a good night's sleep. Tomorrow, before anyone else is awake, I'm gonna show you a few things that I think will help a lot. Okay, buddy?"

The next morning, Jerry shook Charlie awake just as the first rays of the sun filtered through the bunkhouse window. He told Charlie to get dressed and meet him outside. To Charlie's surprise, Jerry led him right past the basketball court, across the dewy grass, and down a small path through the woods that led to the edge of the lake. They sat cross-legged on the dock, Charlie facing the lake. He could see the mists rising off the water, the far shore coming into view.

"Charlie," said Jerry. "You don't have a problem with basketball. You're a good ball handler. But when you're out there with the kids, you freeze. Heck, you freeze whenever the other boys come around, even in the bunkhouse. What are you afraid of?"

Charlie hung his head, said nothing. His eyes filled with tears.

Jerry reached out his hand and grabbed Charlie's face, lifting it. He looked Charlie in the eyes.

"What are you afraid of, Charlie?"

"Ow, you're hurting me. Please, let go." Charlie's voice broke.

"Don't cry. Look at me, right here, right in the eye. Now *make* me let you go."

Charlie's eyes widened. His face reddened. He grimaced, showing his teeth.

Jerry roared at him. *"Make me let you go."*

Charlie's hands shot up, grabbed Jerry's wrist and twisted. His voice came out of nowhere that he knew, loud, clear. "Let me go, you, you, you *fucker*."

"Ow," said Jerry, drawing his hand back. "No fair using fingernails."

"Yes it is. Yes it is. You're bigger than me." Charlie was laughing now, getting to his feet. He started pummeling Jerry with his fists. Jerry put his head down, covering it with his hands.

"Okay, I give up," said Jerry, also laughing.

Charlie backed off. Jerry stood up, gave Charlie a hug.

"Everything's gonna be okay now, buddy. Let's go back and show those wimps how to play ball."

"Yeah," said Charlie. "Let's go get 'em."

Jerry turned to go, then paused and turned toward Charlie.

"Oh, one more thing, buddy."

"Yeah, what's that?" said Charlie.

"This!" He gave Charlie a quick shove, knocking him into the water. Then he dove in after him.

"*Fucker,*" screamed Charlie, gasping, laughing.

Rain Just Falls

Rain, when it falls
Doesn't fall for the flowers
Rain just falls.

—Jimmie Dale Gilmore

"She's such a bitch. Nag, nag, nag, pick, pick, pick. I can't stand it."

I don't mean to be yelling at my therapist, but I guess Velma knows me well enough to understand that I'm not angry at her. I pause for a minute to make sure she's okay, even though she's told me a hundred times that I don't need to worry about her, that she can take care of herself. She gives me that little nod and slightly raised left eyebrow that means "Go on."

"The other day, just like you told me, instead of hanging my head off to the side and fidgeting with my fingers, I stood up real tall and looked her in the eye when she started in on me …"

"Good, good," says Velma.

"But you know what happened? I mean you won't believe this. She starts screaming at me—*'How dare you threaten me!'*—calling me all kinds of names and grabbing the phone like she's gonna call 911 or something. I hadn't even said a word."

Velma's face stays pretty much neutral like always, except now this red flame starts creeping up her neck. "Well, Marty," she says, "I guess that piece of advice kind of backfired on you. How do you feel about that?"

I hate it when she says that. It seems like she says it when she doesn't know what else to say. She knows how pissed I get at my wife. She knows I'd like to smash her in the face, which she fucking deserves. But she also knows I'd never do that—I mean, I'm not crazy. All this stuff about domestic violence never talks about what a guy's supposed to do when he's getting abused. Sometimes right in front of his own kids. Which is why I don't walk. I wouldn't ever leave those kids just with her.

"Not good," I say.

Velma looks at her watch. "We don't have a lot of time left, Marty. Let me summarize what's going on. It's pretty clear that Carol has some serious problems of her own. You've urged her to come in here with you or to see someone on her own, but she just won't do it. So far our strategies for how you should deal with her rage have not paid off. And I agree that leaving her is not a good option at this point— the kids, the current legal scene in this state, and so on. So you're in a real bind. I understand, as much as a woman can, how tough it is for you. But I don't have a lot of ideas left. I was wondering if you'd want to consider working with a male therapist. Someone I would recommend, of course. I'd be happy to …"

I look at my watch. I don't want to hear the rest of it. "Thanks, Velma. I've got to get back to the office, but I'll call you for the information."

I sit in the car for awhile and massage the back of my neck. It's not the first time I've been politely blown off by a therapist. I did have a guy shrink a while back, and he couldn't help either. He suggested I go in the bedroom and beat pillows, which felt sort of good but scared the kids. Besides, I could hear Carol laughing in the other room.

*   *   *   *

After work, I start home. It's cold as hell outside, and I keep thinking about how nice it would be to go home to a warm, loving wife. I guess I thought it didn't matter that Velma gave up on me, but it must. I feel real shitty today, like I can't face going home. I stop at the Come Back Inn for a quick one, hoping to run into someone who can cheer me up. Sometimes the guys from my old job are there, and we get kind of goofy. It isn't even really the booze that makes it easier to face Carol; it's more the good humor that gets carried over from the bar. It's like she can't get to me, at least for an hour or so.

I don't see anyone I know at the inn. I take a draft Heinie's over to a corner table near the jukebox and sit down like I weigh three hundred pounds, which is a joke, because I'm one of the tallest, skinniest dudes I know. Maybe it's my height, I think. Maybe that's why she acts like she hates me all the time. That would explain why nothing I do ever seems to make a difference in how she treats me.

In a few minutes, I am totally back into that stuff Velma calls self-defeating mental chatter. At least this time I'm aware that I'm doing it. Velma's words come back to me: *"Marty, take my word for it. You're a great guy. It's not you. Let go of that kind of thinking."* This helps a little. I look around, hoping some of my old buddies have come in. Then I see this old guy sitting cross-legged on the edge of the step that leads to the men's room. He's smiling at me. I mean not like the way some drunk will grin at you, stupidly. This guy's whole face is beaming at me.

He's kind of fat, but not in a sloppy way. Just chubby all over. And bald, not a hair. He's wearing a white suit and a white shirt buttoned at the neck without a tie. It looks like the kind of suit they wear in places where it's always warm.

I smile back at him, but mine is more like a grimace. He nods toward the chair opposite me and raises his eyebrows. *What the hell*, I think.

"C'mon over," I say, raising my glass to him.

He gets up from that low step like he doesn't weigh anything at all and comes over to my table.

"I'm Marty," I say. "You want a beer?"

"Maybe later, to celebrate your happiness." His voice is very clear, almost like a bell ringing, but soft.

"It's that obvious, huh?" I say. "I bet you're not married."

He laughs, a lot, like I'd told him a really funny joke. "Ah, yes, marriage. So your wife has made you lose your happiness."

"She could make anybody lose their happiness, even you."

He laughs again. When he stops, I say, "But my therapist helped me figure out that my real unhappiness comes from my mother. And she says I probably chose a wife who would also make me unhappy. Something about a 'repetition compulsion.'"

"Ah, yes, therapists," he says. "And mothers. So much to understand." He pauses for a moment, looking down at the table. "Do you need her?" he says.

"Who, my wife? My therapist? My mother? Do I need who?"

"Of course, children need mothers. And fathers. That's why you don't leave the marriage." I wonder how he knows this. "But I am asking about your wife. Do you need her?"

"Jeez, I never thought about it. I guess …"

"Because if you *need* her, my friend, you cannot *love* her." He pauses for a beat. "And perhaps that is why she treats you so badly. Because she needs you so much. Have you noticed how easy it is to be kind to a stranger? We don't need them, you see."

I am getting really confused, then I think I see what he's talking about. "So, if she can only learn that she treats me that way because she needs me, then … but, she'd have a shit fit if I told her that, and she just won't go to the therapist with me …"

"No, no, forget about what she will or will not do. Who knows why anyone does anything? Who knows why the sun shines? Or why it is snowing outside right now?" He waves his hand in the direction of the front window. "We are talking about you. We are talking about how you think she can rob you of your happiness, like a thief. But you are the only thief you need to fear. No one else can take away your happiness. It is your birthright. It is time for you to claim it."

"Wow," I say. "How do you know all this stuff? You sound like some kind of guru." I feel kind of drunk, or giddy, but I notice the bottle is still almost full.

He laughs again. I have never seen a guy so cheerful.

"Oh, please do not curse me with guru status," he says. "I am just like you. Or him, or him, or the other one over there." He stands up, starts to shake my hand.

"Do you have to go already? I bet I could learn a lot from you."

"You don't need me, either, my friend." He puts one hand on his chest, the other on his belly. "All you need to know is in here. And your happiness too, in here."

Outside, it has warmed up a little, and the snow has turned to rain. It is a light, gentle rain. I let it fall on my face awhile. I get in the car and sit there for a moment, one hand on my chest, the other on my belly. I start laughing and head for home.

Midnight Angel

Sherman began his third sleepless night in the ICU with a short, silent prayer to anyone who might be listening and perhaps be able to do something. "Please don't let me die in the night. If I have to die, which, you should understand is not something I want, please let it be in the daytime, surrounded by my loved ones."

Before the evening charge nurse went off duty at eleven, she had offered him a sleeping pill, and he'd refused it. When she asked why, he just shrugged. She didn't seem like the kind of person who would understand his need to remain vigilant.

A few minutes later, Julie the night nurse made her rounds. Sherman realized that she was very pretty. He'd been too sick to notice before tonight. Still, she weighed at least 220 pounds. He supposed that everyone who saw her asked themselves why such a beautiful girl would let herself go like that. Sherman knew she must have her reasons. Julie stood at the foot of the bed, put her hand on his left foot and squeezed gently. She looked right at him, held his gaze without smiling, and asked, "Are you feeling any better tonight, Doctor?"

Sherman could have cried with gratitude. He couldn't know, of course, whether she really cared, but if she didn't, it didn't matter. It was a perfect imitation of caring, and it worked. The others—all the others, doctors, nurses, aides, lab techs—breezed in with a fake smile and a new waitress voice, looking at the chart instead of him and asked brightly, "How are *we* doing?" It made him want to scream.

Sherman managed a smile. "I am feeling a little better tonight. Thanks, Julie. And I'd rather you call me Sherman." He hesitated, then revealed more than he intended. "But to tell you the truth, I'm really scared."

Julie said nothing. She pulled a side chair closer to the bed and sat on the edge of it, her hands open to him, as if waiting for more.

Sherman fought the tears welling up in his eyes. He cleared his throat several times. "You know that guy, what's his name, the *hospitalist?*"

She must have detected the bitterness. "Resnick. You don't like him either, huh?"

Sherman grinned and nodded. "Permission to speak freely?"

Julie rolled her eyes. "Hey listen, Sherman, you can say anything you want." She laughed. "Especially about Resnick."

Sherman laid his head back on the pillow and sighed. "Asshole. Goddam fucking incredibly insensitive asshole! He came in earlier today, when my son and daughter-in-law were visiting. He was frowning at my chart like he didn't know who I was, and he kept flipping back and forth to the lab reports. 'Little problemo here,' he says, still with his nose in the chart and one foot out the door."

Sherman sat up straight in bed and did his best to imitate Resnick's nasal fast-talk.

"'White count was down a little on admission—forty-two hundred, which we attributed to septic shock. The next morning she dropped to thirty-eight hundred, and this a.m., powie, twenty-six hundred. Not a good sign. We may have to ship you to University if she continues to drop.' And then he says … I couldn't believe it … he says, 'Just hang in there, Chief. Try to relax. We'll see which way she's going in the morning.'"

"Oh, God, Sherman, that's awful," said Julie. "He really said try to relax?"

Sherman pounded his fist, the one without the IV, into the bed.

"I could not believe it. I fucking could not believe it. I just went numb all over—you know, like paralyzed with fear. But I had to make light of it for my kids. I told them it was probably nothing to worry about, and I tried to make small talk. But goddamit, I can't get it out of my mind. I keep thinking twenty-six hundred and dropping. My God, acute agranulocytosis. People die from that. No wonder they want to ship me out. Don't die in *my* hospital." Sherman, his anger spent, lay back on the pillow and stared at the overhead fluorescence.

"After the kids left, I asked the charge nurse to page Resnick, to get him back here so I could ask him like what's causing this and what can we do about it and why the hell wait until tomorrow for another white count. But she wouldn't. He's way too busy for that, she told me."

Sherman glanced over at Julie. Her face was red, very red, and her lower lip was trembling. She rose from the chair slowly. At first he thought it was her weight holding her back. Then he realized that she was struggling with something far heavier than her bulk. She paused by the bedside and squeezed his free hand.

"I'll be right back," she said, her voice husky.

While he was waiting for Julie's return, Sherman's body began trembling, first his legs, then a shaking in his chest. He kept his jaw clamped shut. To open it, he knew, would be to risk sobbing like a child.

Julie reappeared at his bedside. Her color had returned to normal. "I called the lab tech at home and told him that Resnick had ordered a stat white count on you. He'll be here in about thirty minutes to draw the blood, then another fifteen for the results. I also asked Melanie to cover my other patients for the next hour."

Julie sat again in the side chair. "We're going to see this through together," she said. She didn't exactly smile, at least not with her mouth, but her eyes were bright.

Sherman let go of a long, ragged breath. His body relaxed. "Thank you," he whispered and for a few seconds he must have dozed, because when he awoke with a start, his mouth was cottony. He sat up and looked at her.

"Julie. My God! I just realized. You could get in big trouble for this. I mean you don't have a written or verbal order from Resnick. What if he finds out?"

"I had to do it," she said. "I'm sick of his arrogance. I've never done anything like this before. I suppose it has something to do with this being my last night."

"Last night?"

She sighed. "I don't know if you want to hear all this," she said.

"Every word," he said. "Please."

Julie stood up. "Look at me," she said, doing a little pirouette in her size eighteen nurse's uniform, holding the hem of her jacket between thumb and forefinger, the rest of her fingers splayed delicately outward like the ribs of a fan. She began pacing as she talked, slowly at first, then with some urgency. From time to time she stopped and faced Sherman squarely, hands on hips, and spoke fiercely, but softly, like a mother trying not to wake the baby.

Sherman listened as if his life depended on it. He knew how to do this, to make everything else disappear from his world except the person across from him, hearing the words, observing shifts in color and tone, knowing what was going on inside her as surely as if it were happening in his own body.

She was getting out of town. She had taken a job as nursing supervisor in a small hospital in Vermont. A place where no one knew her and where she could make a fresh start. Maybe there she could lose weight for real. Maybe then she could meet a guy. She needed to be far from Dad who had loved her too much. And from Mom who had let it happen. And from her little brothers who had made fun of her from the time she was fifteen and the pounds started piling up into layers of protection. And from her stupid, useless therapist who kept telling her if she could only see how beautiful she was, she wouldn't do this to herself. And from her friends who downloaded new diets for her almost daily. And from the other nurses who took advantage of the fact that she had no life and got her to work nights and weekends for them.

The lab tech came and drew the blood. A few minutes later Julie went out to the nurses' station to await the faxed results. When she left, Sherman felt the fear creep back into his belly, freezing him from the inside out. He tried to concentrate on Julie's plight instead of his own, but it was useless. He had to admit he'd rather be fat than dead. He kept his eyes fixed on the door, waiting for Julie to fill it.

Suddenly she was standing in the doorway, as if she had dropped from the sky. She was holding a sheet of paper in both hands, staring at it. Her mouth was open. She looked like a choirgirl about to sing a hymn. Gradually her face broke into a smile. It was the biggest, most beautiful, most welcome smile Sherman had ever seen. She floated toward the bed, her eyes shining. She held the report out to him.

"Fifty-two hundred," she said, breathlessly.

"Fifty-two hundred!" Sherman shouted. "Fifty-two hundred!"

He opened his arms to her, not heeding the IV in his left wrist. They hugged, awkwardly, Julie leaning over the bed, Sherman straining to get his arms around her. She kissed his cheek. He cried a little. Then laughed and cried some more.

"You are an angel," he said. "No—more than that. I'm recommending you for sainthood. How can I ever thank you?"

"Wish me well in Vermont," she said.

"With all my heart," he said.

When Julie left the room, Sherman adjusted his pillow and stretched out on the bed. He knew sleep would come now. But before it did, his mind raced to find a way to express the gratitude he felt in his chest. Julie had saved his life. He was sure of it. If it hadn't been for her, the white count would have gone the other way. It was not something he could tell anyone, but he knew it was true. He would buy Julie a Porsche. No, better, a Mercedes. He would save *her* life; he would move to Vermont, see her every day, help her to lose weight, stay there until she was happily married. Perhaps he would be the one to give her away.

In the morning, when he awoke, she was gone. He smiled. "Be well and happy, Julie," he whispered into the room.

The Letter

David sighed and stared out his office window at the wide boulevard lined with ancient lindens, hoping a decision would come to him. He folded and unfolded the fax he had received from his sister informing him, in the coldest way possible, he thought, that their father had died quietly in his sleep at the age of ninety-two. *I know how old he is,* David would have said, had she telephoned.

He tried to imagine the funeral his sister would arrange. Tasteful, small, and brief. Just as Father would have wanted. Two peas in a pod. Of course, as the oldest child, the only son, he would be expected to say something. He could, with little effort, deliver the expected eulogy. But that would hardly make the trip worthwhile. David, already at the age where mortality is a daily consideration, felt that death was a time for complete honesty.

Have I forgiven him, or have I not? David wondered. He saw himself at the graveside, shading his eyes against the setting sun, saying "I have come here out of respect for my family and to mark the death of the man who was my father, but I am unable to forgive him." No, that would be too harsh, not really the way he felt, and therefore a lie. How about, "I forgive you, Dad. I know you only wanted what was best for me." Another lie. The truth, David knew, was that he hadn't thought much about it over the years, and now, all of a sudden, he had to decide whether to make the voyage to the funeral or not.

If he went, he would have to go alone. That morning at breakfast, Martine had said she had no interest in going. "I never really knew the man, and you have rarely spoken of him" she said. "And your sister has never approved of me—remember your mother's funeral?"

David winced and grabbed his right hip as he pulled himself out of the desk chair. One thing he did know. He would be very uncomfortable during the long, cramped flight if he did not arrange for an aisle seat. That is, if he decided to go.

✳　　✳　　✳　　✳

He was nineteen years old and had never been so excited in his entire life. Only six more weeks of classes, and he'd be off—on the fucking *Ile de France* no less—for a year at the Sorbonne. Junior Year Abroad, the poster had read.

"You bet your ass, plenty a broads," he had said to Hesch, his premed roomate. "I am on my way, Jose."

David reached under the bed and pulled out the old army-green camp trunk, his "file," he called it, where he kept only very important things. The National Merit Scholarship certificate, his high school yearbook, letters from Lou Ann from before the breakup, a poster-sized picture his little sister Marion had drawn for him—she had rendered him about eight feet tall, dressed in whites, with a stethoscope around his neck, and D. Markowitz, MD on the jacket pocket—with HAPPY EIGHTEENTH BIRTHDAY TO MY BROTHER, THE FUTURE DOCTOR, in block letters at the bottom.

It had been really hard to tell Marion that he had dropped out of premed at the start of his sophomore year. Evidently, neither Mom nor Dad had said a word to her about it, nor to anyone else, he guessed. He figured that his mother probably thought the bad news would just go away if she didn't think about it, let alone talk about it. And Dad, "Well," he always said, "the less said the better."

And that is what he said finally after the three-day argument that summer, during which he threatened to stop paying David's tuition if he didn't remain premed, then backed off on the threat a couple of days later, obviously after Mom had worked on him. "So, do what you want; you will anyway. The less said the better."

David pulled the Sorbonne folder from the trunk, took it over to his desk by the window that overlooked Van Am Quad, and reviewed each document word by word.

There was a Xerox copy of the original application he had sent to the committee, "a group of wealthy Francophiles," Robillard had told him, who were underwriting the project and providing scholarships to deserving but poor students. "Poor" being a relative term among Ivy League students, David thought he qualified. His father was, after all, only an optician.

And a carbon copy of the letter of recommendation which Professor Robillard, his advisor and chair of Romance languages, had typed for him. David was almost embarrassed by the superlatives: highest academic standards, an exquisite sensitivity to the subtleties of regional dialects, a consuming passion for the language. David's acceptance into the program was assured, Robillard had told him, and more than likely, he would garner a scholarship.

A transcript of his grades to date, a 3.50 average. Not good enough for Harvard med or even P&S, but who cared now? Better than average for a language major.

And a letter from the committee acknowledging the receipt of his application and informing him that a letter of acceptance or rejection would be forthcoming no later than 31 March.

David placed this last document in a fresh manila folder and set it aside. He carefully returned the remainder of the Sorbonne folder to his "file" and squared the trunk neatly under his bed. March thirty-first had been a Saturday, five days ago. He couldn't have expected the acceptance letter to arrive on the weekend, so he hadn't worried until Monday. Mail was distributed in the student mailboxes every weekday between eleven and twelve o'clock. David had checked the box three times on Monday and four times on Tuesday, each time running down the stairs from his room on the fifth floor of Livingston to the bank of mailboxes just off the main lobby, and then trudging heavily up the four flights, his mind racing.

He decided to take the letter with him to Professor Robillard's class, French Lit 403, and show the professor the "no later than 31 March" phrase, which he had circled. He had been sure Robillard would laugh and say, in French of course, that to a group of ersatz Frenchmen, a firm date is, shall we say, flexible. But there was no laughter, not even a smile. "Come to my office at four fifteen and we shall call Monsieur LaValle together," the professor had said. "I'm sure there is a reasonable explanation."

Seated across the desk from Robillard in his office on the top floor of Hamilton Hall, David had an excellent view of the north side of the campus. Groups of young men, many of them dressed, like David, in hooded duffel coats, milled about at the foot of the statue of Alma Mater, others climbing the terraced staircases leading to the pillared Greek façade of Low Library. To look down on this place, somehow his very own, swelled David's heart. He would miss it next year, he thought, but he would not be lonely, not in France, somehow also his, though he had never set foot on its soil. His mother had been there, he recalled. She had gone to "gay Paree" four years ago with a group of "the girls," and she'd come back entranced, happy for a few weeks at least, exchanging innuendos with her friends who had voyaged with her on the Queen Elizabeth.

Robillard cleared his throat and looked up from the essays he had been grading. "*Eh, bien*, Monsieur Markowitz, let us solve this mystery."

David watched the professor's fingers dialing the number, then played with the fringes of his scarf while Robillard chatted amiably in French with the man known as LaValle. David could not make out LaValle's responses, but he could hear the rhythm and cadence of the high-pitched, singsong voice. When Robillard asked the big question, the "sixty-four thousand dollar question" as David thought of it, David gripped the scarf with both hands and held his breath.

"Robert, I have here in my office Monsieur Markowitz, my best student, who has not as yet received a reply from the committee. What can you tell me?"

David heard a short burst of chatter from the other end of the line, then an interminable silence, then more chatter, though lower in pitch and volume, and slower in pace, without rhythm. He searched Robillard's Gallic face, usually so animated but now set in stone. "*Comment? Oui, je comprend*," he kept saying, until he hung up the receiver.

Robillard spoke now in English. "Your letter of acceptance was mailed to you over two weeks ago—sixteen days to be exact. Did you not receive it? No, of course not; that's why you're here. I don't understand. In the envelope was also a short form, to be signed by you and returned to the committee within three days, indicating your commitment to the program. They waited a week to hear from you, then chose another student, who has accepted. I'm afraid there's nothing to be done at this point. I am so ...."

"Did LaValle say where they had sent the letter?" David spoke in English now also, his voice thin, shrill. "Did he tell you that? Please, please, Professor Robillard, call him back and ask. I beg you."

Robillard turned his palms up and looked sadly at David. Then he redialed the number and, hearing LaValle, asked for the information.

"To your home, your parents' address, upstate," Robillard said. "You must have indicated that address on your application."

"Why would I do that? I'm here. This is my address."

"Well, let's have a look. I have a copy of your application somewhere in the file cabinet."

Robillard stood and searched through the top drawer of the steelcase file near the window. His body blocked David's view of the campus.

"Yes. Here it is. Let's see, under address, second line of the application, you have written 201 Union Avenue, Middle Falls, New York. Your home, yes? So, the acceptance letter was sent there over two weeks ago. Didn't your parents call you? I still don't quite understand how …"

David could no longer hear the words being spoken to him. He thanked the professor, he hoped, and shook his hand, he thought, before he left the office, but he really couldn't be sure. He felt like a blind man. A wave of nausea welled up in his throat. He barely made it back across the quad and into the men's room off the Livingston lobby where he vomited violently. He sat on the tile floor in front of the toilet for a long time, gazing up at the graffiti, some in French.

Later, in his room, he lay on the bed and reread the application. He stared hard at the line bearing his address, as if, given sufficient intensity, it might change. He recalled his trips to the mailbox at Livingston, day after day, and felt humiliated and sickened by his stupidity. He fell asleep in his clothes, his body crushing the application.

In the morning he stared out the window and wondered if he would go to class. It didn't matter; nothing mattered. He caught a glimpse of Robillard, just his black beret, actually, as the professor was entering Hamilton Hall across the quad. Now his question finally registered in David's mind. "Didn't your parents call you?" David added the word that Robillard had politely omitted. Why. Why?

Everyone who knew the optician Morris Markowitz agreed that he was a precise man. A precision lens maker. Always on time. Thorough and organized. When David had been applying to college, Morris had brought home from the office a three-tiered metal desktop file organizer, already labeled in Morris' neat script. The lower tray was for applications completed and mailed, the middle one for interviews and impressions of the campus, and the top level for acceptances. The less said about rejections the better. The dates of scheduled interviews were circled in red on the wall calendar in the kitchen and travel plans were made weeks in advance of those dates.

Morris pored over every piece of mail that David received from colleges. He underlined significant information; any instructions were double underlined in red ink. Morris Markowitz left nothing to chance.

Why? David thought. *Dear God, why? Anyway, it doesn't matter now, there's nothing that can be done. Robillard made that clear. My life is ruined.*

David sat for awhile, until it was too late for class, then he dozed off again. He awoke an hour later, aware of wetness on the pillow under his face. He remembered that he had told Hesch he would meet him for lunch at The Chemists, and a fresh wave of humiliation welled up in his chest. He couldn't face Hesch, or Mike or Sidney or anyone else who knew his plans. And the date, on Friday, with that new girl from Barnard, Marie, who he was beginning to like a lot?— no way.

Tears welled in David's eyes, and a silent wail of protest strangled him. He remembered last summer, alone in his room during a hiatus in the three-day argument, when it looked as though his father was going to win, he had picked up the brass paperweight, the replica of a German shepherd, and heaved it at the family photo on his bedroom wall. He had missed, but the paint and plaster near the photo was chipped and dented. His mother had heard the noise and tiptoed into his room.

"Oh, Davy," she had said, "I'm so sorry."

He had thrown himself on the bed and sobbed into the pillow, but when she had tried to comfort him, he scrunched himself into a ball. "I'll kill him. I'll kill him," he'd said, over and over.

David took a dime from the tin Band-Aid box and went downstairs to the phone booth in the lobby. The booth was directly across from the mailboxes, and David found himself craning his neck to see if perhaps … until a wave of nausea surfaced and he turned to squarely face the telephone. He placed a collect call to Middle Falls.

"Hi, Ma," he said when she answered.

"Davy, darling, I just hung up from Aunt Leah talking about you. Is anything wrong? You never call during the day."

"Ma, is there a letter at the house for me, from Junior Year Abroad?"

"Well, let's see, dear. Your father keeps everything so organized. Yes, here it is, do you want me to …"

"Look at the date of the postmark, Ma. What does it say? Read me what it says."

"Why, my goodness, from New York it was mailed March fifteenth. How silly. I wonder why they didn't send it to you at school, practically around the corner."

"Why didn't you call me when it came, Ma, or send it to me at the dorm? How come you didn't do that?"

"Davy, don't get upset, honey. Your father said there was no sense to it since you'd be coming home in a couple weeks for Easter break, you'd see it then. Right?"

David was silent for what seemed to him a long time. He was aware of not liking the smell in the phone booth. Morning breath, or unwashed body, he couldn't be sure.

"Davy, you are coming home next week. Yes, darling?"

"He ruined my life, Ma. How could he do that to me?"

"You are coming home, dear, aren't you? I've planned a …"

"I don't know, Ma. I don't know."

He hung up the phone, then sat in the booth thinking there must be someone else he should call, but he couldn't think who that might be. After awhile he returned to his room.

David thought about his room at home. The tan corduroy bedspread, the RCA Victrola next to his bed, his neat walnut desk with the leather bound blotter on top, the gold Parker pen and pencil set he had gotten from his aunt for high school graduation. "Don't take it to college with you, David," his father had said. "Not in New York." For a moment he wanted to be there, very badly wanted to be home, in his room.

"It's not my room," David said aloud. *It's his room*, he thought. *And everything in it also his. The bed, the desk, even Aunt Rose's pen and pencil set. Even the clothes in the closet, too big for him, but they're his. Even these clothes,* he thought, looking down at his rumpled khakis, *his, not mine. This room, these books, this typewriter.* He picked up the Band-Aid box and dumped the change on the floor. HIS!

David ran down the hall to the shower room, empty at this hour, and quickly shaved and showered. He returned to the dorm room and dressed in a pair of clean khakis and an oxford button-down. He put on a sweater and the duffel coat and a pair of shiny cordovan loafers. Then he ran down the stairs, raced across 116th Street, and descended into the downtown subway on the corner of Broadway.

David got off the train at Twenty-third Street and ascended the steep staircase. He had to squint against the noonday sun as he strode crosstown toward the river. At the pier, he asked directions to the business office of the Cunard Line. In the office, he waited while the clerk finished a phone call. Then he spoke in French.

"Who do I speak to about getting a job on one of your ships?" he asked.

The young woman responded that positions for college boys were only available in the summer.

"I'm no longer a college boy," David said. "I only look like one."

The clerk directed him to the personnel office down the hall.

"You speak like a Frenchman," she said.

"That's the nicest thing anyone has ever said to me," said David.

∗   ∗   ∗   ∗

David stepped across the room, sat down on the sofa and looked around his office as if seeing it for the first time. He nodded slightly at his desk and bookshelves, the same subtle nod of affirmation he gave to his patients. Lying back on the sofa, feeling the soft embrace of the leather, he looked up at the laminated diplomas lining the wall above the sofa: a master's degree in French lit from the Sorbonne, the MD from the University at Toulouse, Board certification in Psychiatry.

"What's to forgive?" he said aloud.

David stood, opened the door to the waiting room and walked over to the cubicle where Danielle, his receptionist, was typing accounts receivable into the computer. She handed him a sheaf of calls to be returned.

He spoke to Danielle in French. "*Je vais aller aux Etats Unis.* I've decided to go after all. You'll need to cancel my patients until next Monday. They'll understand a death in the family. Please book a flight for me for tomorrow from Marseille to JFK, an aisle seat. And an auto rental at the airport. A return flight home for Wednesday, Thursday at the latest. One needs time, you know, to recover from a trip abroad."

For the Lack
of Anything
Useful

The doctor is smiling. Chip smiles back at him because he's that kind of guy—someone smiles at him, he smiles back. Chip is fifty-eight, but he still remembers what his daddy told him. "Stay away from old barbers and young doctors." This doctor looks half his age. No wonder he's smiling. At that age, Chip had a perpetual erection, a hard-on for life. Always ready to go out and fuck the world. And now? He should have taken Dad's advice.

"Viagra may help. And possibly the condition may improve with time. I mean, it's just six months since we got the little devil out of there. And at least you don't have to worry about having cancer anymore, right?"

The urologist consults his watch. His smile fades briefly and he shifts his weight toward the exam room door. "So, unless there's something else." He takes a step backward and makes a half-salute in Chip's direction. Then he's out the door.

Chip slides off the table and steps quickly into his pants, squeezing his legs together against the urgency in his pelvis. The doctor's head reappears in the door. "See Valerie on the way out, please, Mr. ... um ... Stokes. That's it, isn't it, Stokes? The older woman behind the glass? The billing secretary?" The head disappears.

Chip finishes dressing, dancing from one foot to the other like when he was a kid and didn't want to come inside just to pee. In the hallway, he hurries toward the waiting room and the relief of the bathroom. He smiles to himself, thinking the words *comfort station*. He hears the sound of metal tapping on glass, and someone calls his name.

"Yoo-hoo, Mr. Stokes, I need to see you for a moment."

Chip hesitates. An older woman calling his name always brings him up short. He points to the restroom and signals that he'll be right back. But it's too late. He can feel the warm wetness on his thigh.

∗   ∗   ∗   ∗

Candy had been so sweet and loving right after the surgery. She'd made him rest a lot and busied herself in the kitchen. He was grateful, even though it reminded him of why he'd taken over the cooking years before. After about two weeks, she'd twirled into the bedroom wearing a little thing he'd gotten her at Victoria's Secret the previous summer when she turned forty-five. They'd made love twice when they got back from the store, once before dinner, her sitting on the edge of the kitchen table, him standing, and later in bed after watching a rerun of *Bitter Moon*.

Candy had stood in front of the west window so the afternoon sun filtered through the transparent fabric of the nightie. She'd stroked her nipples in little circles and pouted her lips at him, then wet two fingers with her tongue and slid them into herself, rocking her pelvis and cooing at him.

"Are you ready, big guy. I want your big, hard cock inside me so bad. Oooh, Chipper, come to baby."

Chip had gone over to her and kissed her hard on the mouth, fondled her breasts, and made himself breathe faster. But it was no use.

His dick lay limp in his shorts, and the only desire he felt was to take a leak. He tried to make her come with his hand and she tried to fake an orgasm. She'd said, "That's okay baby," but her face had dropped a mile. That's the way Candy was. She sometimes tried to fool you, but her face never lied.

Lately she'd been gone a lot in the evenings, to some new friends over in East Norville, she said. One night she'd even stayed over, calling him at midnight, sounding really drunk, and saying how she didn't dare drive home. She had come home in the morning and showered and changed her clothes and gone to work.

*   *   *   *

Chip's best buddy Earle told him about it. As if he didn't already know. But now that other people knew, he had to do something. So the next time she came home after staying over with her new friends in East Norville, they had had it out.

"Look, I know you're fucking that guy, that sleazebag, worthless prick from the Seven Eleven. So just admit it. I mean, I can't hardly blame you. I know you need what I can't give you anymore, but I just can't handle it. You fucking him and then coming home and being nice to me and all. And everybody knowing. Everybody but Earle making fun of me behind my back."

Candy cried a lot and said, "I'm in love with him, Chip. I just can't help it."

Chip read her face. "You don't love him, Candy. You love his big, hard cock in your mouth and in your cunt. Now pack your stuff and get out of here. Go live with that scumbag in his scumbag room over the Rite-Aid."

*   *   *   *

"You're a goddam fool if you ask me," Earle had said to him back then. It was shortly after Chip had returned to Eaton Falls from Florida.

Chip's hair was down to his waist, a stringy blond mop falling down from the back half of his head, the front already hairless at twenty-eight like all the Stokes men before him. He'd brought back two kids, Crissy and Jimmy, skinny and curly haired, with wide-set blue eyes like their mom's, eyes that looked like they held the whole Atlantic Ocean in them. They called him Chip-papa. Their mom, Lucinda, had been Chip's fuck buddy for a couple of years, before she decided she had to make the scene in Boulder. She'd told Chip she'd be back for her kids after she got herself settled. He figured a houseboat in Key Biscayne was no place for kids, with him gone shrimping most days. So he'd brought them back to the cabin in the woods off West Falls Road and taken up where he'd left off six years before, running the dairy farm with Dad.

Maybe he *had* been a fool, he thought now, and probably he knew even then that Lucinda wasn't ever coming back for those kids. But now they were all he had, except for Earle, who, after all, wasn't family. Crissy had been coming over every day with food since Candy left him, and it filled his heart to see her and the baby, even though he had to listen to her say all the things she always never did like about Candy. And Jimmy called every week from LA and had sent him an embarrassingly large check for Father's Day.

"Don't go back to the shop too soon, Chip-papa," Jimmy wrote. "Get tons of rest and eat healthy food, which I'm sure Candy will be happy to cook for you (ha-ha)."

✳   ✳   ✳   ✳

The handful of other guys in his class who didn't move on after high school, didn't get the hell out of town like they all swore they would; they lived in trailers tucked off in a corner of the family farm. Like Chip, they worked their asses off all day with their dads and their uncles and any hired men they could afford. Nights, especially the long winter evenings, they drank and did some weed at the Falls Inn or the Red Door. By the time they were twenty, they had wives or live-in girlfriends in the trailer, making babies and thinking about a real house someday. Most of them just added on to the trailers or switched to a double-wide. Houses required time and money.

Maybe it was because he had heard his mom on the phone to Grandma Claudie saying, "That boy can fix anything."

Which he could. Vacuum cleaners, stuck drawers, fractured chair legs. Or maybe it was winning the shop award three years in a row. Freshman year, a knotty pine bookcase; second year, a cherry coffee table; junior year, a maple highboy with drawers that worked smooth as silk. By his senior year he had started on the cabin, taking his time, working nights with lights from a generator. He used pole barn construction, eliminating the need for an excavator and a mason. His dad and his uncles did the wiring and plumbing. Two years later, he had a twelve-hundred-square-foot real house. Lots of windows looking out into the woods on three sides, the south side open to the sun and the valley across the road. He had lived there with Vicki, who had been his steady girl since eighth grade, and worked the farm with Dad. It went sour when she lost the baby. They didn't know how to stop arguing, and she finally left.

"I gotta get outa here," he'd told his dad, and took off for Florida on his Harley. "Don't let nobody touch the cabin," he said.

When he'd been back about six months with Crissy and Jimmy, he met Candy. She was working the checkout at DeVaul's True Value where he'd gone with Crissy to get chicken wire for the goat pen. It was the way Candy talked to the little girl that first got his attention, because he wouldn't have otherwise noticed her with her hair pulled back and that stupid maroon smock they had to wear.

"Your daddy buying this fencing to keep you to home, hon?"

"No, silly," said Crissy. "It's for Chocolate."

Candy turned her palms up and shot a puzzled look at Chip.

"I got her a baby Toggenberg for her birthday. Darn thing don't want to stay put. Keeps jumpin' on the hood of my pickup and dancin' around."

"Oh, my Lord," said Candy. "Your dad got you a *goat* for your birthday. That's the sweetest thing I ever heard of."

He went into DeVaul's the next day on some pretext, roamed the aisles, and waited until no one else was at the register.

"More stuff for the goat pen?" she said.

"Look, um, Candy," he said, glancing at her name tag. "I got two kids and a goat and a black Lab in my house off Falls Road. That's it. I mean, nobody else. I was thinking if you're not busy, maybe we could have a beer at the Red Door tonight?"

When she came in, her hair was down in ringlets around her face, her eyes wide open and sweet. She saw him at the bar and beamed a smile that hooked him right there, even before she slipped out of her windbreaker and her breasts pointed up at him.

✳   ✳   ✳   ✳

He rode home from the doctor's on the new Harley that was supposed to be a replacement for Candy. He still loved tearing up the road, but the thrill was all in his head. He felt numb from the neck down. No racing heart, no blood pounding in his veins, no butterflies in the belly. And worst of all, not a tingle in his groin. He pulled the bike over at the turnoff on Falls Road, parked it, then climbed over the split rail with the Danger No Trespassing sign on it. He half slid down the embankment, grabbing saplings when he could, until he came to rest on the ledge overlooking the falls and the milky turbulence below. He stared down into the gorge. Five seconds, maybe, and it could all be over.

He remembered bringing Candy out there on the back of the old Harley, her hands fondling him the whole ride. He'd wanted to fuck her right there on the ledge, but she wouldn't get anywhere near it. They'd settled for a spot in the woods just off the tourist path, the sound of the falls drowning out her noisy ecstasy. Not that she would have cared who heard.

He picked up a piece of shale and ground it to dust on the rock ledge. When he was done, his hand was bleeding from the sharp edges, and he sucked the blood off and spat it into the falls.

He lay back and stared up at the sun. Useless old man. The same words his dad had used nearly every day, sitting in the recliner on the back porch, his eyes scanning the barnyard and the cow pastures, searching for a piece of his old life.

It was Chip who had found him, a bloody, twisted rag doll lying under the drawbar of the tractor. The old man's shirt had gotten caught in the power take-off shaft of the ancient Allis Chalmers they still used for pulling the manure spreader. It had grabbed his shirt and tossed him around, his head smashing against the frame, his arms and legs snapping like kindling, until finally the shirt pulled loose. He didn't die, but always wished he had. It broke Chip's heart to see his dad sitting in that recliner for four years until—for lack of anything useful to do—he just quit living.

Chip couldn't get anybody to work the farm with him, so after Dad went, he had sold it off to a developer, made enough to keep Mom in a nice apartment in town and some for him to build the shop behind the cabin.

After the surgery, Earle had told him, "You're still the greatest cabinet maker in the county. You can still do that, right? And you got the kids and the grandkid. And you and me can still hit the Red Door sometimes, when Margie turns me loose. Oh, yeah, she said to ask can you come to dinner next Friday. Her sister Mary's coming in from Phoenix. You remember Mary, the crafts lady. You and her talked shop the whole evening, Candy sitting there with her nose out of joint."

Chip sighed, then stood up and dusted off his pants. He hauled himself slowly up the steep incline to the turnoff, sat on the Harley for a few minutes staring at the bend in the road, then drove home sedately, like the old couples on their Gold Wings. He went straight to the shop and uncovered the piece he'd been working on, a reproduction of a bentwood ice cream chair with a cane seat. The lady who'd commissioned it had given him the broken pieces of the original, which had collapsed under the weight of her fat grandson. "Take your time," she had said six months ago, before his life fell apart.

Chip replaced the dust cover, locked the shop and went to sit in the rocker on the back porch of the cabin.

✳   ✳   ✳   ✳

Crissy came into the kitchen empty-handed. She walked over to the cedar picnic set that served as Chip's dining table, where Chip sat now with a bottle of Labatts and a cigarette, his elbow propped on the table, his head propped on the heel of his hand. He raised his eyes when he heard her and managed a weak smile. Crissy took the cigarette from his hand and tossed it into the sink.

"Hey, Chi-pop," she said in an unnaturally loud voice. "Look what I brought you for dinner."

Chip lifted his head and looked to where Crissy was holding empty palms out toward him. Crissy giggled and shot a glance over Chip's shoulder toward the living room.

Jimmy's lime aftershave preceded him by a hair, blunting the effect.

"Surprise! Where's my old man?" He strode over and hugged Chip from behind, kissing the gray stubble on his cheek. "Oh, Chip-papa, I'm here," he said, his voice husky.

Chip untangled his legs from the picnic bench and stood up, shaky on his feet, and hugged his tall son. He took a step back and pulled a handkerchief from the pocket of his sweat pants and blew his nose.

"Look at you," he said.

Jimmy was wearing a dark, expensive suit. An immaculate white shirt open two buttons at the neck, a year-round tan setting off his still unruly mop of blond curls and those ocean blue, wide-set eyes. He glanced at his Rolex.

"I made a res for seven at the Lake House, guys. Pop, you could stand a shave and ... well, you know. You still got that suit from Crissy's wedding?"

Chip drove Jimmy's rental car—a burgundy Crown Vic—the ten miles to Cottersville, then turned north on East Lake. They talked about old times, Chip mostly silent, listening to the kids playing catch-up. He pulled into the forested drive leading to the Lake House and found a space in the lot.

"Lots of high-priced vehicles," he said, looking around. "I don't see nothin' you could get for less than thirty grand. I haven't set foot in this place since the retirement party for Earle's boss. Same suit. Different car."

"Don't be nervous, Chi-pop," said Crissy. "It's outa my league too. But Jimmy goes to places all the time that'd put this to shame. Right Jimmy?"

"Hey, you two. I am so pleased and proud to be here with you. We're gonna have a great evening. Relax and enjoy. Okay?"

Jimmy poured the champagne and lifted his glass. "To our happy little family," he said. "Together again."

"I'll drink to that, but let's not wait another five years," said Crissy.

Chip nodded and emptied his glass. He looked at Crissy. "Okay, missy Crissy, what'd you tell your mister big shot lawyer brother to get him out here?"

Jimmy laughed. "Can't put anything over on you, Chip-pop." He leaned in closer to Chip. "Look, I know you hate to be fussed over, but Crissy was right to call. You don't look good, and you can't just be sitting around all the time. I'm sorry you and Candy called it quits, but you can't let that bring you down. Hell, you're not even sixty yet. There's a lot of women out there. And if you want a bigger playing field, I'll take you with me out to LA."

Chip rotated his champagne glass, studying it. "It's not just Candy," he said. "I just ain't been right since they took out my ... since the surgery." He glanced at Crissy.

Crissy patted his hand. "Keep talking, you two. I need to use the little girl's room."

They watched as Crissy crossed the dining room toward the bar. She stopped suddenly, turned and came back and leaned over the table.

"Don't look now. He's over there, by the entrance, at that big table with lots of men. Your urologist doctor, Chip-pop, I can't remember his name. You always called him 'Dr. Smiley.'"

She turned and walked slowly out of the dining room, her nose in the air.

"Oh, shit, Chip-pop, I get it now. Did Dr. Smiley warn you about the possibility of impotence? I mean, did he discuss it with you before the surgery?"

Chip recognized Jimmy's professional voice.

"Oh, c'mon, Jimmy. Don't go thinking malpractice here. I don't go for all this suing the pants off everybody. Anyway, he did say something about it, offhand-like, you know, a small percentage of cases."

"Right. Of course." Jimmy paused, his fingers drumming the table. He fixed Chip with a steady gaze and spoke slowly. "Did he tell you that in cases like yours, where they catch it early, that at your age, if you do nothing, no surgery, no radium seeds, nothing, there's a better than 50 percent chance that you'd live for years, probably die of other causes before the cancer gets you? Did he discuss that with you? Did he ask anything about your sex life? How important it was to you. Did he encourage you to take time making your decision, to think it over, to talk to Candy, your friends, maybe get a second opinion? Anything like that?"

Chip gripped the edge of the table with both hands, squinted his eyes, and spoke through his teeth, his voice a subdued growl. "What the fuck are you telling me? This 50 percent thing. Are you sure of it?"

Jimmy nodded. "Absolutely, Chip-pop."

Chip's breath made short, snorting sounds. Like a bull. He fixed his sight on Dr. Smiley's table, trying to pick him out.

"No, Jimmy, he didn't say none of those things."

"Calm down, Chip-pop, let me handle this. Which one is Smiley?"

"Red bow tie, brush cut."

"Stay here. I'll be right back."

Jimmy walked toward the table of men. Chip could see his shoulders square under the suit coat. He stopped in front of the doctor and stuck out his hand, smiling, nodding a greeting Chip couldn't hear. Jimmy motioned toward Chip, alone at the table. The doctor smiled and waved. Chip saw Jimmy take a business card from his breast pocket and lean over, placing the card next to the doctor's plate, then speak a few words in his ear. The doctor went pale, the smile dropping off his face like ruined makeup.

Chip couldn't help it. A grin as big as a barn spread across his face. He waved his hand in little circles to get the doctor's attention. So the doctor could see him smile.

*   *   *   *

After the kids drop him off, Chip goes upstairs and puts on his pajamas. He brushes his teeth carefully. He thinks he might have them whitened after all, like the hygienist had suggested. He gets into bed but can't sleep. An old song keeps playing in his head. "You can't always get what you want, but if you try sometime, you might just find …"

He goes downstairs and out the backdoor to the shop, flips on the lights. He unlocks the tool cabinet and snaps the dust cover off the bentwood chair. Glancing around the shop, he thinks he might like to enlarge the space. He could run that idea by Mary over dinner next Friday at Earle's.

978-0-595-45719-9
0-595-45719-3

Lightning Source UK Ltd.
Milton Keynes UK
UKHW010621131219
355323UK00001B/9/P

9 780595 457199